J. S. Cooper

This book is a work of fiction. Any resemblance to actual persons, living or dead, or actual events is entirely coincidental. Names, characters, businesses, organizations, places, events, and incidents either are the product of the author's imagination or are used fictitiously.

Table of Contents

Prologue
Lexi

There's an albatross and a butterfly sitting on a tree branch. And they're whispering, laughing, and chatting voraciously. I'm staring at them wanting to be a part of the conversation. But they can't see me. They can't see me because I'm hidden in a hole in the wall. And there's a wide expanse of ocean between us. I feel afraid because I can see that the branch is about to crack. But the albatross and the butterfly are having such a good time they don't notice. And I try to scream out, "Go back in, go back to the tree, get off of the branch." But no words are coming out of my mouth. And then water starts coming in my hole. And it starts rising. And all I can think about is the branch cracking. And I'm trying to scream to warn them, but no sound comes out. And the water keeps rising. And then I hear the crack and I close my eyes. *This is it,* I think. *This is it.*

But suddenly I feel myself gaining consciousness again. I'm no longer in the dream. I didn't die. It wasn't me who died.

Chapter 1
Lexi

10 seconds. That's how long it took for my world to fall apart. 10 agonizing seconds. Some people say that your life can change in a moment. It can be faster than a blink of the eye. One second, everything is fine—you're going along your merry way, satisfied in the minutiae of your life; even if you're not exactly pumped or overwhelmed, you still exist. Your heart still pumps and your brain keeps thinking and you just continue as you are.
That state of mind can also be known as barely existing. Because that is what it is for most of us. But any kind of existing gives us peace of mind. Well, that peace of mind can disappear in a second. Or 10 seconds. I know that now. Sometimes everything you've ever thought was important can disappear in a moment. And then your very existence is called into question.
"Lexi, Lexi, are you okay?" I opened my eyes to see Bryce standing over me with a worried expression on his ruggedly handsome face. His father stood in the doorway with a slightly anxious look on his; it was the first time I'd ever seen him not looking smug. Maybe he was worried that if I died in his house, he'd have to face my mom again. I knew that was the last thing that he would want. My mom had not taken it well when he had ended their relationship.
"Who died?" I whispered urgently, staring at his dad.
"I don't know exactly." He frowned. "I'm sorry if I gave you the impression that I knew. We have to go down to the hospital to find out."
"Dad!" Bryce barked at his father. "How irresponsible of you. You made Lexi think her mom had died. You should know better."

Mayor Evans looked at Bryce with a murderous look on his face, but he caught himself before he said anything. “The police called me and told me there was a bad accident in town and that there had been a fatality. I don’t know who got hurt. We must go to the hospital.”

“Why do we need to go? You’re the mayor, this is your business.” Bryce frowned. “We have plans.”

“We should go, Bryce.” My voice was slightly louder. “We should go and make sure it is no one we know.” I felt my body tremble as I spoke, but I didn’t correct his incorrect assumption that I thought my mom had died. I felt guilty, but she hadn’t even crossed mind. Luke was all I could think about. I didn’t know what I would do if Luke was hurt. I pictured Luke’s—always friendly and happy to see me—green eyes and wondered if I would ever see the glow of life in them again.

My breath caught and I pinched myself so that I would stop thinking about the worst-case scenario. I needed to distract myself from what I thought was impending doom for not having been a good friend to Luke.

“Catch a falling star and put it in your pocket,” I started singing as I started to get up and I witnessed Bryce and his dad exchange a worried look and then look at me in concern.

“Are you okay, Lexi?” Bryce frowned. “Everything’s going to be ok.”

“Do you see what I see?” I sang, trying to blank his words from my mind. How could he know that everything was going to be okay? Nothing in my life ever seemed to be okay.

“What do you see?” Mayor Evans looked around the room and I laughed, nearly hysterically.

“It’s a song.”

"What's a song?"
"Do you see what I see?" I sang again.
"I don't know what you are seeing," the Mayor answered, irritably. "Let's get going."
"Well maybe you should," I retorted. "Maybe then you'd get a clue, you adulterer." Oops, I had meant to say the last part in my head. I laughed at the look on his face.
"Excuse me. What did you just say to me?" The Mayor advanced towards me and Bryce stepped in between us.
"Dad, this is not the time." His voice was harsh and he grabbed my arm. "Lexi likes to sing children's songs when she feels stressed." He smiled at me, knowingly. "It's the way she copes and it's something I love about her."
My breath caught as he admitted his love for me in front of his father. There was really no coming out of this relationship now. I was partially thrilled and partially scared, but the gnawing in my gut overwhelmed both feelings.
"Come on, Lexi, let's go to the hospital. You can sing in the car."
"Thanks." I smiled at him gratefully and studied his worried face. It seemed to me that Bryce frowned more than he smiled. *Ironic,* I thought to myself. Who would have thought that a gorgeous, rich guy like Bryce Evans would have anything to frown about? Certainly not me. I'd always thought he had the perfect life. Until Eddie killed himself. I had felt sorry for him in a weird way. I hated Eddie, well, somewhat, but I felt bad for what Bryce must have gone through. I knew he had to be hurting and that was why I had started sending the letters.
But that was before I knew the whole story. I hadn't blamed Bryce for what had happened to Eddie then, and I guess I still didn't, even after I knew what had gone down.

At least I didn't think I did. Everything was just too overwhelming for me to think about right now.
The Mayor's cellphone rang again and he whispered into the phone. "Okay. I'm bringing my son and a local girl with me. I'll be there soon."
I saw Bryce's ferocious expression before his dad's words hit me. I thought they were kind of funny: me being called a local girl, like we lived in some sort of small village.
"I asked about your friends from school. They have a listing for one of them in the hospital registry. A Luke Bryan is at the hospital…" The mayor began—and I fainted again.
I never believed that time could stand still before. It just didn't seem possible. I suppose a physicist would say that it defied the laws of gravity. How could it be possible for time to stand still? But I know that it can. When I fainted, I felt like I was in a time warp. Even though I knew Bryce and his father were in the room with me, I felt as though I were seeing them from above. And they were frozen in place. And all I could keep thinking about was Luke. Luke was at the hospital? He was dead, then.
I felt a certain comfort in knowing. A numbing, bone-chilling comfort. The sort you feel when you know your life is going to end, but there is absolutely nothing you can do about it. And then I thought about the day he had bought me a Snickers bar and a beanie baby for Valentine's Day when we were fourteen, because I had been depressed that I had no real valentine.
I had laughed at his poor attempt at a valentine's gift because who gives someone a mini snickers bar? But I had known that it had been the best he could do, with his limited monetary supply. And the fact that he had spent money to try to make me happy had meant the world to me. I could think back to a million other instances when

Luke had done something to make me happy. And many of those instances involved candy bars.
"Lexi, Lexi, are you okay?" Bryce's face was above mine as I slowly opened my eyes as he broke through the time barrier I had created. He looked angry, concerned, worried and I frowned. Why was he frowning? And why was his voice so off-putting? Why didn't he understand that I was freaked out by what his dad had just told us?
"Luke…" My voice trailed off. I didn't want the words to be true.
"I'm sorry, Lexi. But we don't know exactly what happened." He held my hand and I gripped it hard. I had to keep it together. This was no time for me to talk about how much I loved Luke. I hadn't even realized, until this moment, just how deeply my feelings had run. I hadn't realized until it was too late. And Bryce was not the confidante I was looking for. I wanted to call Anna, to see Anna; she would understand.
"We need to call Anna!" I cried out, searching through my bag, wildly, for my phone. "I need to call her and tell her to meet us at the hospital."
"No." Bryce grabbed my hand, panic in his eyes. "There is no need for you to worry her just yet. Let's see what's going on first."
"Okay." I followed him down the stairs. "Okay."
"It's going to be okay, Lexi. Whatever happens, I'm here for you." He pulled me close to him and held me in his arms. I felt cold and numb against him. When he leaned in to kiss me, I pressed my lips together and pulled back from him. I felt his body flinch as I pulled away. I knew I had hurt him, but I couldn't control my body and its emotions.
"I'm sorry," I mumbled, tears welling up in my eyes. "I can't breathe."

"Take a deep breath, Lexi." His blue eyes looked worried and hurt. "And another one ... breathe in and out, in and out."
I followed his instructions and attempted to control my breathing as we got into his dad's car. Part of me wanted to laugh: I was driving in the Mayor's car with Bryce Evans. If I would had told myself in high school that I was going to be in this position one day, I never would have believed it. I was officially dating Bryce Evans and he really seemed to like me, nay—if he was to be believed—he loved me. It seemed unreal.
It should have felt like a fairytale but, oddly, some part of me didn't feel like I was Cinderella. In fact, I felt like I was in a nightmare more than a fairytale. I grabbed a hold of his hand, hoping that I would feel comfort and warmth from having him by my side, but I still felt vacant. It was as if someone had taken out my insides and thrown them away. I didn't want to be in the car with Bryce and his dad. I didn't even want to look at him.
"You're upset because of Luke, Lexi. This will pass. Don't fuck it up," I mumbled to myself as we drove. I pinched my fingers together to try to get some feeling back in my body.
"What did you say, Lexi?" Bryce leaned over towards me. I could see his father watching us in the rear view mirror. I wondered if he knew that I knew what he had done. What he had made my mother do?
"Nothing." I bit my lip hard and stared out of the window. I could taste blood on my tongue, but I felt no pain. In fact, I was starting to feel lethargic. I just wanted to close my eyes and go to sleep. I just wanted to go to sleep and somehow be able to turn back the hands of time. I wanted to wake up three months ago and wished that none of this had ever happened. I would give anything to be able to save Luke's

life. I'd give up the dream of having Bryce love me if he would just be okay.
I felt the warmth of Bryce next to me, I could feel him staring at me with concern and worry and I started to hyperventilate. What was I doing here? I quickly pulled out my phone and dialed Anna's number. She had a right to know about Luke. And I needed to get my mind away from my troubling thoughts.
"Hey." Her voice sounded wary and my breath caught. She already knew, I thought. I then remembered that she and Luke had been planning to hang out that afternoon. Why had I let Bryce talk me out of joining them?
"Hey." I didn't know what to say. I didn't want to voice the words and make them real.
"What's up?" She sounded anxious.
"I'm on my way to the hospital with Bryce."
"With Bryce?" Anna's voice sounded funny. "Is he okay?"
"Huh?" I was confused. "Bryce is fine, he's sitting next to me. Luke is the one who's hurt."
"What?" Anna screamed into the phone and I felt my heart beating fast.
"Weren't you with him?" I asked, confused. Why is she acting like this?
"No, we cancelled our plans for today. I needed to think." Her voice sounds nervous and I wanted to ask her what she wanted to think about. I wanted to ask her why she sounded so funny, but my head is too consumed with everything else.
"Oh?"
"It's been a long week, Lexi. I'm really tired right now." She sounded angry and I didn't know why. My Luke-obsessed brain paused for a moment as Anna spoke. She sounded funny and I wasn't sure why. I felt a pang of guilt

that I hadn't really been around for her much recently.
"So you're with Bryce?" Her words cut me like a knife and jolted me from my haziness.
"Yeah. He's with me. We're going to the hospital." My voice was wrought with emotion. For some reason I felt guilty for being with Bryce, while Luke was at the hospital.
"I see."
"Do you want a ride to the hospital? We could drop by and pick you up." I looked at Bryce to make sure it was okay and I didn't want to ask his father. He is looking at me with a slight frown.
"No, I'll ask my dad." And, with that, Anna hung up. I knew something was wrong, but I wasn't sure what.
"Anna's going to meet us at the hospital." I paused and played with my fingers and turned to look at Bryce. "She sounded funny though. I don't know what's up with her. But she was acting weird. Maybe it was a mistake to call her." My head was pounding even harder now and I rubbed my temples with my fingertips, trying to massage the dull throbbing pain away.
"Then why did you call her?" Bryce sounded annoyed.
"She's one of my best friends, Bryce." I looked at him with a frown. "Of course I'm going to call her."
"Sorry." He looked away from me.
"Bryce is going through a lot right now, Lexi. Maybe you can cut him some slack." The Mayor looked at me briefly and it took everything I had to ignore his words. I felt my heart start to tremble as he pulled into the hospital parking lot and I closed my eyes to ignore my hatred of him and started to pray.
"Please, dear God, please don't let Luke be dead. Please God. Please." I placed my face down to my hands and pleaded tearfully.

"Lexi, he may already dead." Bryce opened the door for me and I can see the worry in his eyes. "Are you going to be okay, Lexi?"

"I don't know if Luke Bryan is the one who died." The Mayor's voice is firm and soft but to me his voice sounds like the wails of a banshee. I wanted to put my fingers in my ears so that I could ignore him but, instead, I overpower them both with my screams.

"What do you think, Bryce? Would you be okay?" I pulled away from him and ran into the hospital. "Where is Luke Bryan? Where is Luke Bryan?" I shouted at the nurse sitting at the front. She looked up at me with a sigh. I suppose she was used to people getting anxious and rude when they came into the hospital.

"What is he in for, mam?" She spoke slowly and patiently. I fixated on her uniform; she was wearing a top with yellow smiley suns on it. *What sort of uniform is that?* I thought to myself. Did she really think that a flowery top was going to make families feel better when their loved ones died?

"He's dead!" I cried out, wanting to slap her in the face for being so calm. Why wasn't she reacting? Why wasn't anyone feeling the same pain and frustration that I was?

"Lexi." Bryce was next to me; I felt his arm around my shoulder. I shook him off of me and he looked at me with a surprised and hurt expression. It seemed to me that he didn't understand how much Luke meant to me and how guilty I felt. If I had just spent the day with him, maybe he wouldn't be dead.

"Where is Luke?" I looked at the nurse with a pleading expression.

"Mam, if you are talking about Luke Bryan, he's on the third floor … but, mam…" she stood up and called to me as I went running towards the elevators. There was nothing

else I wanted to hear from her.
"Lexi wait up," Bryce called after me as I ran into the elevator and I sighed as I pressed the button to keep the doors open for him. "Lexi, you need to relax. Please." He grabbed my hands and pulled me in close to him. "You need to breathe; please, just breathe."
"I can't breathe, Bryce." I felt claustrophobic and closed my eyes. "I feel like the world has just stopped but, for some reason, I'm still alive, still seeing, still feeling, still breathing. But inside I feel dead."
"That's a normal feeling, Lexi." He kissed my forehead and whispered in my ear. "When Eddie died, I felt like I had been transported to a far away planet and had been left there all on my own. I know how you feel, Lexi. Please let me be here for you."
I opened my eyes and saw the tenderness in his, they were gazing into me as if trying to repair my soul. For a second, we were one. We both understood the pain and inner turmoil one experiences when a loved one dies. I knew that he was a kindred spirit and that he cared, he truly cared about me. More than I would have ever believed before. More than I would have ever hoped for.
"Thank you, Bryce." I spoke softly and squeezed his hand. I needed him to know that I wasn't pushing him away. I just needed this time to be by myself, to come to terms with the grief that was consuming me and burning a fire in my soul.
"I'm looking for Luke Bryan." I ran up to a doctor who was walking past me. "Please, please, tell me where he is."
He looked at me with a funny expression and pointed down the hallway. "Go past the desk, look in the third door on the right; I think he's in there."
"Okay. Thank you." I started running down the hall, but stopped when I got to the desk. I was scared. I didn't want

to go to the room. I wanted to postpone the moment. I didn't want to accept that he was dead. Maybe if I just went home, I could pretend, pretend that he had just gone on a trip to Boston and that he would be back. I could wait for him to return. Maybe, if I prayed hard and long enough, he would come back. Maybe it was time for me to start believing in miracles. I turned around, suddenly feeling calm and grabbed Bryce's hand.
"We can go." I smiled at him. I felt as if I were walking on air.
"What's going on, Lexi? You haven't been in the room as yet?" He frowned at me and I reached over and rubbed his temples.
"You must stop frowning, Luke."
"I'm Bryce."
"Oh, sorry." I bit my lip. "Shall we go and get a shake?"
"Don't you want to see Luke?" Bryce came to a halt.
"I don't want to see." My eyes widened in fear. "I don't want to see him. Please."
"Lexi…" Bryce's voice trailed off as his phone rang. "It's my dad." He put the phone back in his pocket.
"You can answer it."
"I'll call him back once you have done what you need to do, Lexi. I'm sure he just wants to rush home to get ready for another date."
"He's still your father, Luke."
"I'm Bryce, Lexi."
"Sorry, my brain is a little fogged up right now."
"Let's go in the room." He turned me around and we walked until we reached the third door on the right. "Do you want me to walk in with you?"
"I think I should go in by myself," I whispered. Bryce nodded and stepped back and I took a deep breath and

walked in the door. I was overwhelmed as soon as I set foot inside the room. It was crowded and I felt my blood pressure soaring as I scanned the room to look in the beds. And then I saw him. My Luke. And I fainted once again. Only this time I didn't see Luke's childhood face. This time I was in a meadow and there were blue butterflies flying around saying my name, "Lexi, Lexi, Lexi." And I thought to myself, *I never knew butterflies could talk.*

Chapter 2
Bryce

I don't like hospitals. They make me think of death. And only death. When I was in boot camp, we had all talked about our least favorite spots. The guys had laughed when I had told them that I hated hospitals most of all. *Even though babies are born there*? Someone had asked me one could dreary night when we wanted our minds to be on anything other than the war. *I've never met a baby,* I had told him, *not one that I've held and bonded with.* I didn't associate hospitals with babies. Just death. And I've known too many people who have died.
I kept my back against the wall as I waited for Lexi. I didn't want to see her face as she saw Luke's limp, lifeless body. I didn't want to see the heartache and crushing pain in her eyes. I couldn't bear to see it. She shouldn't have to go through this. I'd brought my curse to her. I felt my fist clench and I released it, tapping my foot instead.
"OMG, is she okay?" I heard a little kid scream and I ran into the room. Lexi was lying on the ground, lifelessly. I felt my heart clench. She had fainted again. She must have seen him then. It was true then. Luke was dead. I should have felt relief, but all I felt was an incredible sadness pass through me.
"Shelby, go and get the doctor so he can make sure she is okay. She hit her head when she fainted." The voice was concerned, husky and familiar. I looked up and froze as I saw Luke standing in front of me.
"Okay, Lukey, I'm going now." The little girl ran past me and out into the corridor.
"Gimme a hand won't you, Bryce." Luke nodded towards Lexi and we lifted her up and put her on an empty bed.

"What are you guys doing here?" Luke frowned at me.
"We came to see you."
"How did you know I was here?" He looked a little nervous and I wondered what he was doing in the hospital.
"My dad ... wait ... how comes you are alive?"
"How comes I'm alive?" Luke laughed. "Do you want me dead or something, Bryce?"
"No, no. Of course not." Which was true. I didn't want him dead. I just wanted him to be out of Lexi's life.
"So?" He questioned me.
"My dad told us there had been an accident, a fatality, and then he said you were in the hospital. We just assumed there was a connection."
"Sorry. I'm still alive."
"I didn't want you to…" I trailed off as Lexi groaned. I leaned down and looked at her. "Hey, are you okay?"
"I thought I saw Luke." She smiled, weakly and I nodded to her other side. She turned her head and saw Luke and I saw the shock and happiness in her face. Her eyes lit up and I felt a jab of jealousy.
"Luke, is that you?" Her voice was breathless as if she thought she was talking to an angel.
"Yes, Lexi."
"Am I in heaven?"
"No, Lexi." He laughed and I groaned inside. "I wasn't in the accident. I don't know who died, but it wasn't me."
"Oh thank God." She sat up and grabbed him. "Don't you ever do that to me again, Luke Bryan." She buried her face in his chest and I looked away, heart pounding. *So this is what jealousy feels like,* I thought. I'd never felt this odd sensation of mind-numbing hurt and pain before; the hollow thudding in my chest was a foreign experience and, as I watched Lexi and Luke out of the corner of my eye, I

felt like I wanted to throw up. Never had a sensation overwhelmed me as much as it did now. And then she pulled away from him and turned around and smiled at me, and that fleeting green monster disappeared from my body. "He's alive, Bryce." She beamed at me, tears of happiness flowing from her eyes.
"I see that." I knew that words sounded dry coming out of my mouth, but I didn't know how to fake a relief I didn't really feel. It wasn't that I wanted Luke to have died. Far from it. I just didn't feel any particular way, now that he was alive.
"I should call Anna, tell her you are okay." Lexi avoided my eyes and spoke directly to Luke as she walked out of the room. "I'll be right back."
"Okay." Luke's voice and mine echoed out at the same time. I felt a wash of gut-wrenching fear in my stomach, it was becoming a familiar feeling every time Lexi mentioned Anna and I wasn't sure how much longer I could put off telling her. I wanted us to move on in our relationship, but I didn't want to do that with any secrets. I needed to know she accepted me a hundred percent for who I was and what I had done.
"The doctor is on his way, Luke." The little girl walked back in the door and smiled shyly at me. She had a bandana on her head and gaunt cheeks. I smiled back at her, taken aback by the way her big, blue eyes seemed to engulf her face.
"Thanks, Shelby." Luke gave her a quick hug. "Now get back into bed and rest."
"But I want to play charades. You promised."
"I promise to play if you rest some more."
"Promise?" She got into the bed and put her thumb in her mouth.

"I promise."
"Okay." She leaned back and pulled the bandana off of her small head. I tried to keep my smile plastered on my face as I stared at the top of her head. She was bald. I'd never seen a little girl who was bald before. It suddenly reminded me of my surroundings.
"I don't mind if you stare." She turned to me with a small smile. A smile that tugged at my heartstrings.
"Sorry, I didn't mean to stare," I mumbled, embarrassed.
"I have cancer," she said, matter-of-factly.
"I'm sorry."
"Don't be sorry. I got to meet Luke," she mumbled, sucking on her thumb.
"Oh?"
"He…"
"I'll explain more to Bryce, Shelby. You just sleep now. You've had too much excitement for the day."
"The girl fell." Shelby looked at us with worried eyes.
"Yes, but she's okay now."
"Good. She was pretty." And, with that, Shelby closed her eyes. Luke pressed his hand to her forehead and stood there for a while, watching the girl.
"Is she your sister?"
He looked up at me in surprise and he stared into my eyes with a searching look. "No." He spoke slowly, frowning.
"Your niece?"
"No."
"Cousin?"
"She's not related to me." He ushered me towards the door. "I met her through volunteering."
"Oh, okay." It figured that Luke was a do-gooder. He was literally better than me in every way possible. I suppose it had to with our DNA, his parents must have both been good

stock, while I had one parent that was likely related to Satan himself.

“Let’s make sure Lexi is okay.” Luke’s voice was firm and I followed him out of the room, stopping to look back at the bed before I walked out. Shelby looked so tiny and frail lying there. I felt my heart skip a beat as I stared at her peaceful face, sleeping. Life was so unfair sometimes. Such a small child should be running around and having fun—not sleeping in a hospital room. I wanted to ask Luke her story. For some reason I was drawn to this little girl.

“Everything okay, Lexi?” Luke grinned at Lexi and ruffled her hair. “Did you tell Anna I’m okay?”

“Yes.” She rolled her eyes. “She, like me, was ecstatic to hear the good news. But she will kill you if you ever put us through that again.” She wiped her eyes. “I didn’t know I could cry that much.”

“But I didn’t put you through anything.” He laughed easily and I wanted to punch him for laughing like everything was okay. Didn’t he realize what he had put Lexi through?

My phone started ringing again and I groaned as I saw my dad’s name on the screen again. “I am coming, Dad. Luke is okay. We are just—”

“—Bryce, you need to come downstairs and meet me in the lobby.”

“Lexi and I will be there in a minute.”

“Come alone, Bryce.” His voice caught and my heart skipped a beat. I’d never heard my father sound this serious and emotional before.

“What’s up dad?” I sighed into the phone, annoyed. I saw Lexi and Luke exchange a glance and look at me as I talked and I rolled my eyes to indicate my annoyance at my dad’s call.

“It’s your mother.”

"What about her?"
"She's not well." He paused and took a deep breath.
"What do you mean?" The blood drained from my face. "What's wrong with her?"
Lexi clasped her hand to her mouth and looked at me with wide eyes.
"Come down, Bryce. Please."
I hung up the phone and looked at Lexi with bleak eyes. I felt as if my body had just caught on fire. "My dad wants me to go downstairs to talk. Something's wrong with my mom."
"Your mom?" Lexi's smile dropped from her face. "Do you want me to come with you?"
"No, no. I'll go. I'll be right back." I knew I was walking because I was getting closer and closer to the elevator but I couldn't actually feel my feet moving. The out-of-body sensation reminds me of how I felt going into combat the first time. It was surreal and deafening at the same time. As I got into the elevator, I watched as Lexi and Luke stood there together, watching me. It was a curious look; one I wasn't used to. They looked like they pitied me. I'd never had anyone pity me before.
"Bryce." My dad rushed up to me as soon as I got out the elevator and his eyes were red. That was even curiouser. He looked like he had been crying. My dad never cried. He had no need to—everything in his life was perfect. Just perfect.
"Where's mom, dad?" The words echoed in my ear and I looked around to see who had spoken.
"She's gone, Bryce."
"Gone where?"
He put his head in his hands and I think he held in a gulp. It was all quite strange. "Bryce, it was your mom in the accident."

"No." I pulled his hands away from his face. "Stop lying."
"Bryce, mom has died."
"No." This time my voice was firmer and louder. "No, she cannot be dead. She was going to leave you."
"Bryce." He looked at me with a strange pain in his face. "I'm sorry."
"It's not me you should be apologizing to, dad, it's mom. Go and find mom and apologize to her."
"I'm sorry, Bryce," he whispered.
"No. No you're not sorry. Go and tell mom!" I shouted and pushed him. "Go and tell mom what a shitty husband you've been. You're lying. She's going to leave you."
"I know." His voice was quiet and a tear fell from his eye. "She had me served with divorce papers."
"What?" I hadn't known that my mom was actually strong enough to follow through with her words. I hadn't expected her to really leave my dad. "What are you talking about?"
"Bryce, we can talk about this later. Do you want to see your mom before she is sent to the funeral home?"
"She's not dead." I sob. "She can't be dead."
"I don't know what to say, Bryce." He tried to put his arm around me and I shrug away from him forcefully.
"Don't you dare touch me." I pushed him hard, wanting to harm him in some way physical. "Where is she?"
"Let's go and see her."
"I want to see her by myself." My head is pounding as if someone is hitting me with a hammer over and over again. "I need to see her by myself."
"Just come with me. I'll take you there and leave you alone with her."
I counted the tiles as I followed my dad and try to walk on every other tile without touching the grout lines. I can only walk on the navy blue tiles, not the white ones, I tell

myself. If I touch the white ones, even by mistake, the game is done and I lose. I can't touch the white ones. I jump a little bit to make sure that I don't even let my heel touch the white ones. But then my dad stopped right in front of me and I stumbled and land right in the middle of a white one. I wanted to scream. And I wanted to punch him hard. He made me lose the game.

"She's in there." He tapped on a door and I stood there for a moment before going in. I heard the television playing some gameshow and I turned around and snarled at him for playing such a horrible joke on me. My mom wasn't dead. Maybe she was just injured. I could hear the TV playing. I bet she was happy to have some time to herself in the hospital, before coming back home to cook countless dinners. I pushed open the door with a smile on my face, ready to cheer my mom up. I had to blink to become accustomed to the darkness of the room. The curtains are drawn, the lights are off and the only light is that the TV is emitting.

"Mom, do you want me to turn the light on?" I fumbled around, looking for a light switch. I turned it on and the room was filled with a bright fluorescent light. I understood why the light had been off now. "Mom?" I stared at the bed and see my mom lying there with her face looking straight up. As I walked to the bed, I can feel every nerve ending in my body alert and waiting for a command.

"Mom?" I stopped at the edge of the bed and look down. Her face is pale white, almost grey, with a tinge of blue.

"Mom, do you want me to go home and get your blusher?" I knew she would want to put a little makeup on her cheeks.

"Mom." I touched her cheek slowly, praying silently for her to open her eyes and shout "April Fools."

I put my fingers on her neck to see if I felt a heartbeat. And, at first, I think I am positive that I felt one. It's beating quickly and I breathe a deep sigh of relief—but then I realized it's my own heartbeat I am counting. I put my fingers under her nostrils to see if any air is coming out and I just watch her face. My brain already knows the truth that my heart doesn't want to accept it. I closed my eyes for a second and think about her happily cooking for my party—she had been so alive, so carefree, so determined. And I was pretty sure she hadn't been on anything. She was getting better. I knew she had been getting better.

"Oh mom." I fell to my knees and placed my head on the bed sobbing. "Oh mom, how could you leave me? I need you mom. I need you to be here for me. We can do this together. I support you. I support you mom. Leave dad. I'll come with you. We can do this. Oh mom. I love you. I love you so much. Mom, wake up. Wake up. Mom, wake up." I screamed sobbing at this point. No death has ever affected me this much, this deeply, this painfully. Every atom of my body was crying out in hurt.

"I'm sorry, Bryce." I felt my dad's hand on my shoulder and I don't say a word. I hadn't even heard him come in. I wanted to scream at him, tell him it should have been him that had died. I wanted to tell him how much I hated him. But I didn't want to do it in front of my mom. She wouldn't want that. She had loved my father, for all his flaws, even though he had broken her. She had loved him.

I stood up and stared down at her face—so beautiful, even in death. I bent forward and kissed her cheek for the last time. "I love you, mom," I whispered in her ear and walked out of the door. I used my sleeve to blow my nose and wipe the tears from my eyes. "Sorry, mom," I said to the air. I knew my mom had always hated me using my clothes as a handkerchief.

"Bryce, we need to make some decisions." My dad addressed me and I looked up at him with hatred in my eyes.
"How did she die?"
"She was in a car accident." His eyes were cold as he responded to me. I guess, when we were alone he didn't have to put up a pretense.
"She died from a car accident."
"She wasn't in her car. Someone hit her as she was getting into the car. They lost control."
"I see." I didn't see. What sort of senseless driver could do that?
"They were texting," he sighed. "They took their eyes off the road to text and, when they realized they were about to hit the car in front of them, they swerved and hit your mom."
"So they took a life to avoid a fender bender," I said, bitterly.
"I'm going to work on passing a no texting while driving law."
"So you're already thinking of the job again?"
"Bryce, please. We can't continue like this. Your mom wouldn't want that."
"You don't know what she would have wanted." I walked away from him and back to the lobby. I wanted to go to Harpers creek. In fact, I needed to go to Harpers creek. I needed to be alone. I needed to punch the ground and to scream. I needed to think.
"Do you really think your whore of a girlfriend is going to be there for you more than me, Bryce?" My father caught up with me and I turned around and right hooked him.
"You shut up, you son of a bitch." I hit him again. "You fucking prick; it should have been you in there."

"Bryce, Bryce, he's not worth it." Lexi's voice distracted me from hitting my dad again and he backed away from me as she ran up to me.
"He's an asshole, Lexi." I looked at her with wild eyes. "My mom is dead because of him."
"I didn't kill your mom, Bryce."
"You pretty much did," I shouted, suddenly overwhelmingly tired.
"Come on, Bryce." Lexi took my arm and led me to the side of the room. "It's going to be okay."
"It's my fault, Lexi," I burst out, looking at her caring face. "It's because I'm evil. Everyone dies around me."
"No, Bryce, you can't think that."
"Eddie died, Simon died, now my mom."
"You aren't responsible for anyone else's death, Bryce." She reached over and looked in my eyes. "You're a good guy, Bryce."
"I slept with Anna." The words spurted out of my mouth without control and I cringed at the look of shock on Lexi's face. But I still continued, "the night of the party I slept with Anna. I was fucked up on alcohol and pills; I didn't know it was her. But I didn't stop it. I fucked up, Lexi. And now, now I don't know what to do. I don't know how to make it right. I don't want to lose you. I love you, but I can't do this anymore. I can't keep it in. I can't pretend everything is okay. I love you. I want to be with you. But I'm not a good guy. I'm just not a good guy. I can't live like this anymore. I can't keep being punished. I don't want anyone else to die."
I know I should given her the chance to respond to what I'd just said, but I didn't want to think about it anymore. I just wanted to drown in my sorrows. I just wanted to get away. I ran back to my dad to ask him for the car keys. I'm

surprised when he gives them to me right away. I looked back at Lexi and her big, brown eyes are still wide with shock. I wanted to tell her I loved her and beg for her forgiveness, but I know that I don't deserve it. Instead, I run out of the hospital and to the car. "It's going to be okay." I heard my mother's voice whispering in my ear as I drived and I cried, silently. *Nothing is ever going to be okay again,* I thought to myself.

Chapter 3
Lexi

I tried to avoid Luke's gaze as he walked up to me. I didn't want to see the "I told you so," in his eyes. I felt cold inside. I was in shock. How could Bryce have slept with Anna and, more importantly, how could Anna have slept with Bryce? She was meant to be my best friend. She was my oldest friend. She knew my secrets. She knew how much Bryce meant to me—how much he had always meant to me. I can remember the first time I ever told Anna about my crush on Bryce.

We had gone to our first high school football game as freshmen and we had played a game called *If not him, then who?* We basically chose a famous actor and said if we couldn't date him, we would pick and then choose a guy from the football team. We couldn't really see what the guys looked like in their uniforms, but we had been lucky to have gone to Jonesville High (where football reigned supreme) because the school created a leaflet with all the players' photographs on it.

"Okay, if not Matt Damon, then who?" Anna had giggled at me as we sat huddled together in the bleachers, ignoring the game.

"Oh, it will be hard to match up to Matt Damon." I had surveyed the leaflet and had immediately been struck by the confident and handsome gaze of Bryce Evans. "Him."

"Ooh, he's cute."

"He'll be my pick every time," I laughed. "He could be an actor. He's hot."

"I think this Eddie guy is cuter," she had laughed and pointed to a skinny looking guy.

"No way." I stared out onto the field to see if I could see

my new crush and, as luck would have it, he had scored the winning touchdown at that moment. “Touchdown for number 34, Bryce Evans.” The announcer had screamed through the speakers. “Jonesville High is riding high, folks.”
Anna and I had grinned at each other and she had cocked her head. “I bet you’re his good luck charm.”
“Yeah right.” I had rolled my eyes but felt a warm glow inside. Maybe she was right. He had scored the winning touchdown after I had chosen him as my favorite and been looking for him on the field.
“Wouldn’t it be great if we could date Bryce and Eddie, Lexi?”
“Yeah. It would be.” We both sighed and walked to the parking lot, so we could wait for Anna’s dad to pick us up.
“Lexi, are you okay. Lexi?” Luke’s voice interrupted my reverie and I felt him poking my arm.
“Sorry what?” I looked up at him in confusion.
“I said, are you okay?” The concern in his eyes took me back and I blinked.
“Yeah. I was just thinking.”
“He’s not worth it you know, Lexi.” His voice was low and agitated. “He’s always going to be the bad guy that hurts you. You deserve better than that.”
“You don’t know him like I do, Luke.” I sighed, too overwrought to have this conversation now. “You don’t know what he’s been through.”
“We’ve all been through stuff, Lexi.” His voice sounded angry.
“I know.” I stared at the top of his head. His hair needed cutting. Maybe I could convince him to give me a shot at playing barber again.
“Lexi, you deserve better than him.”

"Luke, I don't want to talk about this now."
"But I do, Lexi." His voice was insistent. "Look at me, please."
I slowly looked into his eyes and his eyes seemed to want to tell me a message. A message I didn't want to hear. A message I didn't want to see. I was too confused. Too hurt. Too wounded.
"I love you, Lexi." He grasped my hands and pulled me towards him. "I love you so much, Lexi and I can't stand to just watch you get hurt. I can't stand to see your heart torn to pieces over some guy who doesn't care two shits about you."
"Luke," I began, weakly; my brain was scrambling for something to say.
"Lexi. Can't you see that we're meant to be together?" He grabbed my hand and placed it over his chest. "Can't you feel the beating of my heart? A heart that exists just to love and be loved by you."
"Luke, please." I cried and pulled away. I just can't deal with this right now.
"Why can't you answer me, Lexi?"
"Anna wants to date you. I can't," I whispered.
"Anna just slept with your boyfriend, Lexi."
"No." My breath catches and I close my eyes. "She can't have."
"Bryce told you himself."
"Why would she do that to me?"
"I don't know, Lexi."
"I'm her best friend." I looked at him wildly. "I drive her to work every day."
"People do funny things, Lexi."
"She knows how I feel about him."
"What about me, Lexi?"

“I can’t do this right now, Luke. I’m too confused. Please.”
“You’re never ready, Lexi.” He sighed. “Do you want a ride home?”
“Please.” I looked down, embarrassed.
“Come. I’m parked around the corner.”
We walked in silence to his car. I felt ashamed of myself. I didn’t know what to say, what to feel. Luke had been my best friend for years, yet I felt so distant from him. So alone. I have no one now I thought to myself. I still couldn’t believe Anna had done this to me. How could she have done this to me? I felt a fire in my belly, a tingling pain of betrayal. But, as Luke drove me home, I also felt confusion. He loved me? A part of me was overwhelmed and exalted at the news. But everything was so complicated. I didn’t know how to feel. I didn’t know how to act. Bryce needed me. He was the one for me. He was my soul mate. And soul mates stuck together through thick and thin. I knew how much he had been through. I couldn’t leave him now. He would have no one. I couldn’t leave him with no one.
“I suppose you’re not going to answer me.” Luke spoke right before we pulled up to our street. “I suppose you want me to pretend that this conversation never happened.”
“I don’t know what to say, Luke.” I looked at him and sighed. “I’m just really confused.”
He laughed, a deep, rough guttural sound and I looked at him with sorrow. I wished he hadn’t told me how he felt. I wished he had kept it to himself.
“I’m sorry, Luke.”
“Don’t be sorry.” He parked the car and looked at me. “Did you know that I’m an albatross, Lexi?”
“Sorry what?” I frowned confused. Had Luke lost it?
“One day you’ll understand.” He smiled at me, sweetly and

took my hand. "You will always be my best friend, Lexi and I am always here for you. Please remember that."
"I'll call you." I got out of the car with tears in my eyes. The words didn't seem adequate for the emotions running through me. They didn't adequately impart everything I wanted him to know. I wanted him to know that he was a part of my heart. That when I had thought he was dead, I had wanted to die as well. But I couldn't say those words. I didn't want to give him false hope. Not when Bryce was still in my life. Bryce was the one I had been waiting a lifetime for. Love didn't always come easy, but I had prayed for this opportunity. He was the one. I had always believed he was the one.
I didn't look back at the car as I opened my front door. I didn't want to see Luke watching me. I didn't want to feel even guiltier than I currently did. I didn't think I could survive more pain and sorrow in my heart right now. I was too tired. So very tired.
"Lexi, is that you?" My mom came down the stairs with a frown on her face. "Where have you been?"
"I was at the hospital, mom."
"Oh, okay. Did you want to go to get something to eat?"
"Not really." *Thanks for asking if everything is okay,* I thought to myself.
"Shall we order in a pizza then, instead?"
"I'm not hungry, mom."
"Maybe we can ask your young man Luke to come over as well."
"How many times do I have to tell you? Luke and I are not dating, mom!" I screamed as I ran past her on the stairs.
"There's no need for your attitude, young lady."
"Shut the fuck up." I whispered, under my breath.
"What did you say to me, Lexi?" She chased me up the

stairs. “Do you know how much I have sacrificed for you?” she screamed at me and I crouched back, scared she was going to hit me. “You are such an ungrateful cow, I gave up my whole life for you.”

“I just want to go to my room, mom.” I knew better than to respond to her words. I had learnt that a long time ago. “Can I just go to my room?”

“Go to your room. I’m going out.” She turned away from me and I ran into my room and locked the door. I tried to control my breathing by rubbing my head. I have a splitting headache and I know that I should take a tablet. I walked to my door slowly and open it one inch at a time so as not to alert my mother. I tiptoed to the bathroom and paused as I heard the almost silent sobs of my mother coming from her room. I’m rendered immobile for a minute, feeling my heartbreak once again.

I wanted to go to her and hold her. But I knew from previous experience that, if I were to do that, she would soon turn on me. Her emotions were as temperamental as the weather and I knew that the smartest thing to do was to stay well away from her when she was in one of her moods. She went from happy to angry faster than a cheetah chasing its prey.

I walked quickly and grabbed the Motrin that was in the cupboard and scrambled back to my room. I could see the light on in Luke’s room as I opened my door and I wanted, more than anything, to be able to shout out to him and ask him to come over.

“It’s just you now, Lexi.” I looked at myself in the mirror and frowned. I didn’t want to be this person anymore. Hiding in my room. Feeling sorry for myself. Allowing the misery of others to dictate my life. What had I done that was so wrong? Absolutely nothing. I pulled out my phone and contemplated calling Bryce to make sure he was okay, but there was one phone call I had to make that was even more important.

"Lexi, hey." Anna sounded cheerful as she picked up the phone.

"Hey."

"You don't know how happy I am to hear Luke is okay."

"Oh yeah?"

"What's wrong, Lexi?" Anna sounded unsure of herself. "You sound funny."

"Did you sleep with Bryce?"

"Wait, what?" I hard her gasp and I knew in that second that it was true. There was a part of me that had hoped that Bryce was lying. And that he was even more twisted in the head than I had thought. I wanted to believe he was sicker than Anna.

"How could you, Anna?" My voice was low, and I allowed the hurt to come through.

"I didn't mean to, Lexi," she whispered.

"You have known how long I've loved Bryce. How long I have waited for this moment."

"I just…"

"Why did you choose this moment to be the worst best friend ever?" I cried out, angry and hurt. "How could you, Anna?"

"It wasn't just me, Lexi. *He* slept with *me,* too."

"Yeah, after you drugged him," I spat out.

"I didn't drug him," she cried out. "We made love, Lexi. Bryce and I made love. I didn't make him do anything."

"Sex isn't love, Anna." I was deliberately cruel. "Just because you were a slut doesn't mean he loves you. He loves me. He wants to be with me."

"Who doesn't want to?"

"What?" My voice rose. "Is this because Luke told me he loves me? Are you that jealous of me?"
"Luke loves you?" I heard a sharp intake of breath and, for a moment, I felt a shred of sympathy for her.
"I can't believe you did this to me, Anna. How could you?"
"You've never been here for me, Lexi. Do you realize that? I'm always here for you. Always listening. Always sympathizing. Always there, in the background for you to talk to. But are you ever there for me?"
"What are you talking about, Anna? I have been here for you our whole lives."
"No you haven't!" she screamed. "When Eddie died, did you ask me if I was okay?"
"Anna, why would I ask you that?" I frowned into the phone.
"I know he tried to rape you, Lexi and I hate him for that. But I loved him. I was trying to help him."
"What are you talking about, Anna? You barely knew him." And then I remembered our game again. I had chosen Bryce and she had chosen Eddie. I thought back to our sophomore year, when Anna had first decided to volunteer at the pound, she had done so because Eddie had been doing community service there. And when she had dragged me to see the Red Hot Chili Peppers. I hadn't minded because Bryce had been there, it hadn't even crossed my mind that Eddie would have been there as well. "Why didn't you tell me, Anna?" I whispered into the phone in shock. "You were in love with Eddie, weren't you?"
"Can you believe you're supposed to be my best friend and you never knew?"
"You never told me, Anna."
"I tried to tell you all the time, Lexi. But you don't care. You only ever seem to care about yourself and what's

going on in your life."
"That's not true, Anna." I bit my lip. "You're my best friend. I'm always here for you."
"No. No you aren't." Her voice went silent and we sat on the phone just listening to the silence. "Do you remember when I got the job as a tutor? I told you how excited I was because I thought it would give me a chance to get to know Eddie better."
"Not really," I sighed, not recalling the conversation.
"But then you told me you were trying to establish a relationship with your dad. And I knew how important that was for you, so I didn't mind that you had changed the subject on me, even though I had been trying to talk to you about Eddie."
I sat on the bed, my head still pounding, even though I had taken the headache tablets. "I don't remember, Anna."
"And then, a couple of months later, Eddie and I went to lunch together. He wanted to thank me for helping him get an A and I was so excited and I called you to get some help picking an outfit."
"You and Eddie went to lunch together?"
"You told me you were too busy to talk, because your mom was having one of her episodes. You told me you would call me back. But you never did. And I called you back that evening and your mom said you were having a sleepover at Luke's."
"I'm sorry I forgot to call."
"It's not just that, Lexi. Do you know how many times you've invited me to a sleepover at Luke's?"
"It's not my place to invite you to Luke's, Anna."
"It doesn't mean that you couldn't have asked him to invite me. How many times have you done that?"
"Anna, I don't…" My voice trailed off as I heard her crying

on the other line.
"I'm really sorry, Lexi. I really am, but I don't think I'm the only bad friend here. And if you can't see that, well, I don't know what to say."
"Anna, I don't understand, we were always in this together."
"No, we're not, Lexi. You always say that we're the invisible girls but we're not. I am. I'm the only one who is invisible. No one sees me. Everyone sees you. Luke, Bryce, even Eddie. They all wanted you. Not me. No one sees me. I'm fed up of being a nobody."
"But Anna—"
"—I know you think it's shitty that I slept with Bryce and maybe it was. But I'm so fed up of this life. I'm so fed up of being the sidekick, here just to see you find love. What about me? When's my time?"
I lay back on the bed, unsure of what to say and then Anna hung up on me. My eyes were dry, but I felt like crying. I wasn't even sure what to think or feel about what she had said. Nothing could excuse her for sleeping with my boyfriend, but maybe she was right. Maybe I had been a bad friend to her. Maybe I had taken advantage of her friendship. Anna was just always there. I always knew I could count on her when I needed someone to talk to.
I sighed as I realized that I hadn't really been there for her as much as she had for me. Even when it came to her liking Luke, I was pretty sure that she had a crush on him, but I'd never asked her. Never tried to pry and see if my thoughts were correct. And I wasn't sure why. Maybe I was scared that she and Luke would get together and I would be the odd one out. Because that was what she was. She was the odd one out in the friendship. Or maybe they both were. Maybe I was the sun to their planets. Everything in my life

revolved around me. Maybe the real issue was that I was selfish.

I wanted to call Luke. I wanted him to tell me that I wasn't selfish. That I was a good friend. A good person. I had always thought that Anna and I were in it together. We were the invisible girls. But maybe only one of us was really invisible.

It's hard when you recognize that you've been a bad friend. It's really hard. I felt like I had blown my friendships with Luke and Anna. It seemed like there was no way to redeem myself now. No way at all. I dialed Bryce's number, hoping he would answer the phone. The phone went to voicemail and I tried to ignore the pain I felt at his non-answering. I knew he had to be at Harpers creek. It was his go-to place, just like it was mine. But I didn't know if he wanted to see me, I knew his demons must have been eating him alive right now.

More importantly, I didn't know if I wanted to see him. How could he have cheated on me? Already? It was something that I had never thought could happen. I was going out of my mind as question after question ran through my head and I knew that I had to get out of the house.

***

Driving around Jonesville is something I have been doing since I have been able to drive. I like to watch people walk down the street as I drive past them, listening to music. It soothes me and makes me feel like I'm on top of the world. Even though I'm only driving a Ford Escort, I still feel like I have it made. At least, more than the people who are walking do. I know that, perhaps, some of them are walking because they are exercising, but I like to think it's because they don't have a car. It's an odd way to feel good about oneself, but I guess I'm a bit of an odd girl. That day, though, I drove aimlessly, changing from radio station to radio station, nothing quite catching me: not the top 40, not the country music and not even the 80's and 90's hits. And I didn't even bother looking to see if anyone was walking down the streets. That didn't matter.

"Is Your Life In Tatters?" read the sign that caught my attention. I pulled over, parked and got out, hoping that I wasn't about to venture into some scientology group or cult. I got out and saw that the sign pointed to a small cottage and the words 'Psychic—Come and have your reading today' were hanging above the door. I've never gone to a psychic before. I've never really cared to—I mean, who wants to fork over their money to someone who will just BS them? I don't have a lot of money and I'm certainly not going to give it away to someone who's a charlatan but, that day, I decided why the heck not?

I walked up to the door, slowly, trying to talk myself into going in. "If it's over $20 you will walk out, Lexi," I told myself. I had nothing to lose. Everything in my life was falling apart.

"Hello, my dear." An elderly lady opened the front door and I peered at her in surprise. She was dressed normally, no veil around her face, or mountains of jewelry.

"Uh, hi." I looked around, quickly. "I think I'm lost. Sorry." I made to turn around, but her next words stopped me.

"It's okay, dear, I've been expecting you."

"What?" I felt a little scared at her words. "You've been expecting me?"

"Yes, dear." She smiled at me, warmly. "Why don't you come in? Let me offer you some tea."

"Well..." I paused, not wanting to be rude.
"You won't offend me if you go, but I do think I can be of some help to you in your dilemma, my dear."
"Hmm okay?" Was she for real? How did she know I had a dilemma? But then I thought back to her street sign. Obviously, anyone who was stopping for that sign was having issues—anyone could guess that.
"I have chocolate chip cookies as well, Lexi."
My mouth dropped open as she said my name and I stared at her, suspiciously. What was going on here? "How do you know my name?"
"All will be explained, my dear, all will be explained." She opened the door wider and I decided to follow her in. She seemed so short and frail that I knew I could beat her in a fight if she tried anything funny.
"Would you like tea or coffee?"
"Coffee, please."
"Have a seat, I'll be right back." And, with that, she waddled off to the kitchen. I looked around the room curiously as she left. It was light and airy with two big, yellow couches. I was sitting on one of them next to an old sleeping cat and it appeared as though she had been sitting, knitting, on the other couch. It looked like she was making a scarf, and I wondered who she was making it for. I looked at the walls and there were lots of pictures of different lighthouses, but no family photos. I wondered if her family had disowned her because she was crazy. I mean, she didn't seem crazy, but if she was passing herself off as a psychic then she had to be.
"I brought some gingersnaps and chocolate chip cookies for you, my dear."
"Thanks." I studied her face as she offered me the plate of cookies. She had to have been about seventy-five. Her hair

was pulled back in a bun and was pure white; she had sparkling blue eyes that belied her age and quite a lot of wrinkles on her face. She looked as normal as anyone's grandma would look and not at all like I would have expected.

"The coffee will be ready soon, dear."

"How did you know my name?" I leaned forward, anxious to understand how she knew.

"Well, dearie, I had a dream."

"A dream?"

"I know you young folks don't believe in religion and what not these days, but have you ever heard of Joseph?"

"The father of Jesus?"

"That's good, my dear," she smiled at me, happily, "but no."

"Oh."

"Joseph was the son of Jacob. He used to interpret the Pharaoh's dreams."

"The Pharaoh? Like Tutankhamen?"

"Read Genesis, my dear, you'll understand."

"Uh, okay." Maybe this was a religious cult after all.

"I had a dream about you, Lexi. I always seem to have a dream about the girls who are coming to see me."

"Only girls?"

"No. But more likely than not, it's a girl." She smiled and stood back up. "The pot must be ready. I'll be right back. Milk and sugar?"

"Yes, yes please." I watched her walk out of the room and felt a strange calmness in me. My brain was telling me to run, but I felt safe and curious. I wanted to know what else the lady had to say.

"Smile, dear, it's not nearly bad as all that." She brought a tray in and I jumped up to help her. It looked too heavy for

someone of her stature to carry.
"Shall I take it?" I offered a hand and she shook her head.
"I may look old and frail, but I'm still a very sprightly woman."
"Okay." I took the cup she offered me and added three spoonfuls of sugar to my cup. "You don't look like I expected you to."
"Oh?" She laughed. "I suppose you expected a mystical looking lady in a dark room with a big crystal ball?"
"Something like that." I laughed, embarrassed.
"We're not all frauds, my dear." She coughed. "Though some of them do have far-sight. Though they shouldn't be using it."
"What?" I frowned.
"Nothing to concern yourself with, dear. I suppose you've come for some answers?"
"Yes, yes please." I nodded, eagerly, grateful that she was going to supply me with a way out of this mess.
"Your dad isn't a bad person."
"Ok, wait, what?" I frowned at her. "That's not why I'm here."
"We don't always know the root of our issues."
"I'm here because of a guy…"
"It's always about a guy." She smiled at me, gently. "At least, that's what our heart tells us. Inside our soul we know differently."
"No, I'm here because of these two guys." I tried to interrupt her.
"He loves you, in his own way of course. It was your mom he was weary of. She's not well."
"I don't know what you're talking about." My chest was pounding and I didn't want to hear what she was saying. "I want to talk about my boyfriend, well, I think he's my

boyfriend."
"You went to look for him, yes?" She peered into my eyes with a soulful expression and I felt myself shiver.
"Yes, how did you know that?"
"Parents are so important in our lives. You know, there are many people who shouldn't be parents. Many people who don't have the emotional capabilities to look after themselves are now having kids. They—"
"—Sorry to interrupt, but how does this affect me?" I frowned at her and she sighed.
"Sorry, dear, I sometimes go off on tangents. Let me focus on why you came. You're at a crossroads in your life, Lexi. This is an important moment. And it's not because you feel yourself to be the latest damsel in distress. No. It's because you realize that the you that you have been portraying is not the you, you want to be. Sometimes we see ourselves as a martyr, and we live our lives as if we are fighting the fight of the world. Unfortunately, many of us are just fighting the fight of our hearts, of our dreams, of our wishes.
"You know, I want to tell you a story about a man I once knew. His name was John and he was a baker. He had the biggest bakery in town. And every day he would bake fresh bread. And he would deliver it to all the families in his town, and these people all happened to be the men and women that he went to church with. And, every Sunday, he would provide free bread to the church and he would tithe ten percent of his earnings. Every single week."
"Uh, okay."
"Yes, John was a good man. In fact, everyone in town loved John and respected him. And he loved them as well. There was nothing John would have changed in his life, asides from the fact that his town sat next to a very poor village. The people in this village would follow John on his

bicycle as he delivered his bread and he always complained to the families he delivered to that the people scared him. They were disheveled, dirty and smelly. He was always worried that they would try to jump him and steal his bread."

I tried not to yawn as she continued telling her story. I had no idea what she was talking about, but I didn't want to be rude and interrupt.

"And, one day, one of the men from the next village threw a rock through the window of his bakery and stole some bread and pastries. John was devastated and went to the police station to press charges. He couldn't believe that something like that could happen to him and his store, as he was the nicest, and most generous guy in the town."

"But if he was soo nice, why didn't he give them some bread?" I asked.

"He didn't know they were hungry."

"But they were obviously poor. I mean they came from a poor village and they looked disheveled."

"John didn't see that. All he saw was some people following him around as he did his job."

"Didn't he ask them why they were following him?"

"No. He never asked them why they were following him. He didn't care why they were following him. He was more concerned about his own wellbeing."

"So, what happened next? What happened to the guy who stole the food?"

"The guy who broke the window and stole the food was put in jail and, a few days later, his baby daughter died."

"What?"

"He had been stealing food because his family was malnourished and had no other way to get food. He had been following John around for years; yet John had never once spoken to him, never once asked him if he was okay or needed anything."

"That's horrible." I felt tears well in my eyes. "I thought he was meant to be a good person."

"In his eyes, he was the best human being he thought he could be." The old lady paused to sip some coffee. "But he never looked past himself."

"What happened next?" I leaned forward. "Did John feel guilty? Did he go and help the man's other kids and wife? Did he start to give free food to the people in the village."

"John got a guy so that he wouldn't be bothered by the people in the village following him."

"Oh." It was not the ending I had expected or hoped for. I felt disappointed. "So what was the point of the story? John didn't learn anything. He still never helped those people."

"That's because John never had a moment where he realized that he was self-absorbed and that there was another reality outside of his own."

"I see." But I didn't really.

"Lexi—you realize that, even though you've been hurt, there are others who are also hurting and that, perhaps, you have been blind to those hurts."

I nodded my head slowly at her words, shocked that she seemed to see inside the depths of my soul, that I was hiding, even from myself.

"It's hard to acknowledge that we aren't who we've always thought we were."

"I've tried to be a good friend…" The words tripped from my mouth. "I don't even know how to feel. I've been betrayed, but I also feel like a betrayer."

"Life is never black and white, my dear."

"And what makes it worse is that it was my best friend who betrayed me. She slept with a guy I've been in love with,

well, I think I love him, for years. How could she do that to me?"
"And that makes you feel angry. And confused. But you are more confused because there is another man who holds your heart. And, once again, your friend is a part of that equation."
"How did you know that?' My mouth dropped open again and she smiled at me.
"I'm a psychic, dear." She put her coffee cup down and leaned towards me. "The simplest path is to follow your heart, my dear."
"But I don't know what my heart is telling me." I closed my eyes. "I think I love them both. Bryce has been my dream man for years. I never thought I had a chance with him. He's handsome, he's charming, he's broken and he needs me. I feel like I'm all he has.
"But then there's Luke. He's been my best friend for years. My shoulder to cry on. My laugh buddy. The only one who has always been there for me. No matter what. He has always been there for me. And he loves me. I think, I think he's always loved me. I just never wanted to see it. I didn't want to ruin our friendship. I didn't want to lose him.
"And then there's Anna. My dearest, wonderful Anna. My oldest friend. I thought we were like two peas in a pod. I always thought that we were the same—just different bodies. But we're not. I know that now. I've never really listened to her. I've never really tried to figure out what she wanted. I just always assumed everything was great because, in comparison to me, I thought it was."
"And why is that, Lexi?"
"She has a dad who loves her. He'll do anything for her. She's wanted and loved. Her parents tried for ten years to get pregnant with her. She was their miracle child."

"How does that make you feel?"
"I'm jealous." A tear ran down my face as I stared at the wall, unseeing. "I just want to be wanted. My mom, my mom is crazy. I love her but she's crazy. I had hoped my dad wanted me, but he didn't care. I went to see him and he pretended he had no idea who I was. He dismissed me. I'd always hoped that he would want to take me in. That he had missed me so much that he wanted me to be in his life." I sobbed as the memories of my dad's dismissal played out in my head. " I just wanted him to love me."
"He does love you, Lexi."
"No he doesn't," I sobbed.
"He loves you in the best way that he can. Did you know he was addicted to meth?"
"What?"
"And he's been in and out of jail. He did the right thing by you, Lexi. It may not seem that way now. But your life is better without him in it."
"It just hurts inside. I don't know why I'm so unlovable."
"Oh, but Lexi, you're far from unlovable."
"It doesn't feel that way. I just feel so empty and lonely inside."
"You've had a lot to deal with. And a lot you've never dealt with."
"I just don't know how."
"You're not alone, you know." She smiled at me gently. "Your loved one. He has a similar feeling in his soul. A hollowness he's never shared with anyone."
"Who? Bryce?"
"You'll know when the time comes. You're not quite as alone as you think. There are many secrets in families that some of us would never even guess existed."
"I guess." I sighed, suddenly tired. "So what do I do now?"

"I can't tell you what to do." She sat back and shook her head. "That's not what I'm here for. I can't make your decisions for you."
"But can't you tell me what the right decision should be?"
"I will tell you what you need to hear. I want you to make the decision that makes you happy. I want you to go outside and listen to the birds chirp and whistle, follow the light of the sun, touch the fragrant petals in my garden and breathe in the fresh air of nature. I want you to listen to the beat of your heart and then I want you to close your eyes. Go and lie in a meadow and stare at the sky. The answers will come."
"Uhm, okay." I frowned. I didn't want to tell her that she hadn't been very helpful but she really hadn't. Next thing she'll be telling me to listen to the whispers of a butterfly.
"Life is not quite as complicated as we try to make it, my dear. And friendships are never broken until we cut them."
"I see." I stood up, slightly frustrated. "How much do I owe you?"
"Nothing."
"If you're sure." I walked towards the front door, feeling guilty and she patted me on the back and smiled.
"And dear, only the black swallowtails are worth listening to."
"Uh, okay." I walked out the door confused, wondering if perhaps she had dementia and if I'd been part of some elaborate ruse. As I walked to my car, I decided to pull out my phone and looked up black swallowtail on Google. I might as well know what she's talking about.
"A butterfly." I said aloud to myself. "It's a butterfly." I bit my lip and looked back at the house, wondering if she was a mind reader. I didn't even know her name. I sat in my car for a second, unsure of where to go. I felt like I had been in

her house for a few hours, but when I checked the time it had only been forty-five minutes. I rolled my window down and let the cool breeze flow into my car. I took a deep breath and let the scent of the road take over my senses. And then I started my car. I knew where I wanted to go. I wanted to go to Jonesville High, back where everything had started. I wanted to go to the football field.

***

I was alone in the field, feeling a little bit like a fool. I was twenty-two years old and lying in the middle of a high school football field. As I lay there, I realized that so many of my problems were related to Jonesville High. And that, perhaps, was a problem in of itself. I was twenty-two now. I shouldn't be living in my past. I shouldn't be living for the dreams and memories of my high school self.

I closed my eyes and I breathed deeply and then stared up at the sky. It was an off-white blue grey. It looked like it was going to rain, but I continued to stare until an overwhelming sense of wellbeing filled me. I felt light and happy and alive. I felt like there was nothing too big that I couldn't handle. It was time for me to grow up. I was responsible for my own happiness in life. I couldn't place blame on anything else. It was like my dream of being an actress.

I had always said I never really wanted to be an actress, but it was just a lie. I was scared of people laughing at that dream, it seemed so lofty and unachievable. So I pretended I only wanted to be one to be admired. I hadn't even been brave enough to try out for the drama club in high school, even though I had gone to every play, secretly and by myself. That was a dream that I had never told anyone. Because I was scared. But I didn't want to be scared any more. I didn't want to be unsure.

And then his face popped into my head. And he was smiling at me. He was telling me that this was the moment I had to make a decision. And I could see the exact crinkle of his eyes as he smiled at me. That pure, genuine, loving smile. And I wondered how I'd never noticed the pain in his eyes before. I had studied them so much. But all I had seen was his façade.

And I thought of the morning and the anger and happiness I had felt being around him. And the confusion. And the pain. But, more than the confusion and the pain, I felt the happiness and the love. And I knew. I had always known. He was the one that I loved. He was the one that I was made for. He was my one and only. He always had been. I couldn't believe that I had ever questioned it.

I jumped up and ran. I ran faster than I had ever run before. I had to go and see him. I needed to tell him that, no matter what happened, we could work through it. I needed him to know that I was here for him one hundred percent. The past didn't matter. It would never matter. Jealousy had no place in our lives. Both of us would have to get over our insecurities.

I knew that, together, we could get through anything. I'd never felt so excited or scared in my life. I knew that he might not want to hear it. I wasn't sure where his head was after everything that had happened, but I had a feeling I knew where he was and I was going to try my hardest to get him to talk. I wanted to get him to understand why I had been the way I was earlier. I knew I had hurt him. I knew he was hurting now. I didn't know if I could take away his pain completely, but I could try to absolve as much of it as

possible.
I tried not to speed as I drove, but I was anxious and excited. I saw the sign for Harpers creek and I gripped the steering wheel with a thudding heart. I had finally made a decision; a decision that I hadn't consciously thought needed to be made in my whole life. It had taken being told that Luke had died to make me realize the depth of his importance in my life. And then, hearing him tell me that he loved me had broken me and I had wanted to scream at him, "Don't do this, don't do this. Not now. I can't take this!" And it had killed me to see the pain in his eyes. But I also knew that Bryce was in need of my love more than anything in the world. My Bryce. The guy I had spent my whole high school life loving.
I gulped as I saw the second sign for Harpers Creek and my heart felt like it was going to break out of my chest. I felt excited and sad all at the same time. I knew that my decision was going to end up breaking someone's heart.

Chapter 4
Bryce

There's something about the sound of silence that makes you feel comforted. Maybe it's because when we're in silence we don't have to bother with the externalities around us. In war, the sound of silence is never a good thing. It means we are waiting for something big to happen and we don't want to be heard. The eerie sound of silence while you are at war is usually followed by a deafening bellow; a scream or an explosion and then all that calmness vanishes. The calmness vanishes and chaos ensues.

Silence can indicate impending doom, but as I lay here in the most deafening silence, I wasn't scared. The doom had already happened. My life was already over. I was a zombie now. Living, but not really. I was one of the walking dead. I laughed to myself at my joke. Maybe there was a reason I enjoyed watching the show so much on TV. Maybe I knew that I was soon to be a part of them; one of the tribe.

I walked to the riverbank and saw the little bubbles indicating that fish were swimming by—how easy their life must be, I thought. How simple and refreshing. Maybe I could catch a few and take them home for my mom to cook. I was about to go to my car to grab a hook, but then I remembered my mom wasn't here any more. She wasn't going to be frying up any more of the fish I caught. She wasn't going to be there to ask me what food I wanted her to prepare for a dinner party, we weren't going to watch Jeopardy together any more, or to talk about football games. I laughed as I thought about how much my mom used to love to talk about football. More than any guy I ever knew. I think it was because her cousins had all been into football, so she had grown up talking about football every

holiday season.
She'd been so proud of me as the quarterback. She'd come to every single game. She didn't miss one. Not a one. But she had never been disappointed when I had turned Notre Dame down; even though I knew she had been excited to come up to the games. She'd always told me that whatever I wanted to do was fine by her and that she would always love and support me. And she had. She'd loved me through everything. And she'd cried with me when Eddie died. It was as if she had known that I felt guilty. She had been home the night Eddie and I had fought. She'd seen him running and crying, heard me banging the walls. And then, he'd died. And I had broken down. But mom had been there for me.
"Say hi to Eddie for me, Mom." I whispered to the river. Maybe my mom was telling Eddie how sorry I was about what happened. Maybe they were catching up and laughing about all the things he and I used to do to cause trouble when we were youngsters. It was thoughts like that that made it easier for me to breathe. To exist. I wanted to go home and grab my bottle of pills. I knew they would help me. I knew that they would numb the pain and the crushing fire that burned inside of me. But I resisted. I had to resist. I knew that if I didn't start resisting the urge to pop a pill, I'd be seeing the other side of a grave myself. And I knew that I didn't want that. Not now and not that way.
I'd lost everything today: my mom, Lexi, my self-respect. I could still see the shock in Lexi's eyes as I had told her about Anna. She had been so hurt. I wanted to tell her it meant nothing to me. That Anna had been nothing. And that she had made my heart soar with love and lust with just a touch of her lips against mine. The feel of her skin had sent a fever up my spine, that hadn't been quenched with

our mating. I longed to touch her, to feel her, to consume her. I wanted her right now. I needed her here on the riverbank, to be with me, to love me, to heal me.
I froze as I saw a deer run out to go and drink some water. He paused as he saw me and our eyes connected. There was a passing of some deeper emotion that slowed between us and it was as if we were communicating subconsciously. I willed him to come over to me. But, as I took a small step closer, he ran away from me. I laughed as he ran. Even the deer knew that I was the scum of the earth.
I sat back on the grass and looked at my phone to see the time. I had three missed calls: one from my dad, one from Lexi and, surprisingly, one from Anna. I hadn't expected Anna to call me. I suppose she was upset that I had told Lexi what had happened. Another selfish act I suppose.
I put my phone away without calling any of them back. It still hadn't quite hit me that my mom was dead. I couldn't believe that I wouldn't see her smiling face again. She wouldn't be coming up to my room to tell me that dinner was ready. She wouldn't be sending my care packages. And I wouldn't be helping her to move out, to finally live her life, away from my conniving dad.
I had wanted her to win so badly, to defeat him—to make him look like a fool to the whole town. And now that would never happen. She'd never get to meet my kids, or to gush at my wedding. I'd never see her again. The tears ran from my face and I tried to stop them. I was a man. I shouldn't be crying this much.
My phone started ringing again and I grabbed it from my pocket to see who was calling. I was so shocked to see Luke's name that I answered it.
"Hello?" I kept my voice low so he couldn't hear the emotion.

"Is that you, Bryce?"
"Yeah. What's up?"
"I'm sorry about your mom."
"Thanks." I wanted to tell him to shut up but I was too tired.
"I know you think my words are baseless but they're not. I knew your mom quite well. I saw her at the hospital a lot."
"At the hospital?" I frowned. "Why was she at the hospital?"
"Sorry, I thought you knew. She volunteered there, in the kid's ward."
"Oh, I didn't know."
"Yeah, she and I both had a special bond with Shelby."
"That's nice." My heart dropped as I thought about the little girl with cancer. I didn't want to think about another girl dying.
"We both took an interest in Shelby because she's an orphan, you see."
"That's sad." I didn't know what to say. I just wanted to get off the phone. "But why did you call?"
"I guess you wouldn't call her an orphan per se," he continued. "Her parents are alive, but she was given up."
"Man, that sucks," I sighed.
"She's been at the orphanage since she was born. Once families find out she has cancer, they don't want to adopt her."
"That's shitty."
"But we think she's in remission now."
"That's great," I said, truly happy to hear some good news. "That's really great."
"Your mom was going to try and adopt her."
"What?" I sat upright and my hand grasped the phone tighter.

"She was waiting to do it after she left your dad. She hadn't told Shelby yet, but she had discussed it with me."
"Why didn't she tell me?" I frowned. "I didn't even know she volunteered."
"She started coming to the hospital when you joined the marines. She said she felt like God would protect you if she spent time with other children. She worried about you so much."
"I didn't know." Why hadn't she told me?
"She was going to adopt Shelby?" My voice held disbelief.
"I don't know how to say this, Bryce, but Shelby is your sister."
I dropped the phone onto the ground and tried to picture the little girl's face. There had been something so familiar about her. "I want to see her."
"You can come with me tomorrow if you want."
"Yes. I want to come." I paused. "How do you know I'm her brother?"
Luke sighed before speaking. "I replaced the orphanage's computers and software a few years ago. That put me in contact with a lot of personal information."
"So you know about my dad and Lexi's mom?"
"Yes." His voice was clipped.
"But she doesn't know." It was a statement and not a question.
"I wanted her to tell me about the affair when she was ready."
"But Shelby's her sister as well."
"It wasn't my place to tell her," he sighed. "She doesn't even know that I know."
"Are we going to tell her?" I didn't know if I could drop another bomb on her.
"Shelby would love to get to know you both. She's a

wonderful young girl."
"So you know my sister better than I do." It felt weird saying the word *sister*. "She's going to be okay now, right?" I knew it was selfish of me but I didn't know if I could handle getting to know her, only for her to die.
"She's okay now, Bryce. She's in remission," Luke sighed. "She's a survivor, Bryce. She's a good kid. She needs a brother to love her."
"You've loved her like a brother though, haven't you?"
"I love her." His words were firm and wistful. "Your mom loved her as well. And Shelby loved your mom."
"I'm glad." I smiled, a big, wide, true smile. "I'm glad she had someone in her life who made her happy."
"She was a good woman. Everyone in town loved her." Luke paused. "She wouldn't want you to blame yourself, Bryce. It's not your fault. Just like Eddie's death wasn't your fault."
"You're a good guy, Luke," I sighed. "Thanks. I'll meet you tomorrow at the hospital?"
"Yeah, I'll see you there around noon."
"Okay, I'll see you then." I jumped up, suddenly feeling alive. I had a sister. A little sister. It didn't feel quite real. She could have been my daughter. I laughed at the irony. Maybe I'd have a kid soon. Maybe I could convince Lexi to forgive me and we could start a family. And I'd be a better man. I'd be a stand-up guy. A family guy. I'd spend the rest of my life atoning for my sins. I'd be the guy my mom wanted me to be.
First, Lexi and I could get married. We could get housing at Notre Dame and I could get a degree, maybe I'd become a teacher. Or maybe I could go to theology school. Spend my life in service to God. And then, when we graduated, we could start a family. And buy a house. We'd be a real

family. I knew that Lexi would like that. We'd be happy. I would spend the rest of my life showing her how much she meant to me. I had messed up with Anna, but I wasn't going to make the same mistake twice. I would prove to her that I was a good man. That the guy she had loved in high school was the real me and not a figment of her imagination. I could be that guy. I could grow up. I could be the man she wanted me to be, that I needed to be.

I grabbed my phone to call her. I wanted to hear her voice. I wanted to hold her. I needed somebody right now. I knew she wouldn't mind if I held her in my arms and cried. I just needed to be with someone. I needed to feel complete. I needed it more than I needed oxygen to breathe.

Chapter 5
Lexi

My phone battery died as I rounded the corner. But I didn't care. I didn't want to talk on the phone. I needed to see his face and talk to him in person. I finally arrived and parked my car next to his. This was it, then. I took a deep breath and shook my hands out.

"Hey, you."

"Hey." I looked up and saw him standing in front of me. "I didn't even see you there."

"I guess you need to pay more attention to your surroundings, then." He laughed and I breathed a sigh of relief. Everyone was normal. As I had thought it would be. As I had known in my heart it would be.

"Yeah, I don't want any scary bears coming after me."

"Especially not if you've eaten any honey lately."

"Or chocolate."

"Or salt and vinegar chips."

"Or McDonalds fries."

"Or Whopper Jrs., without the pickles."

"And added cheese."

"Oh yes, we can't forget the added cheese." He grinned and I pulled him close to me. I saw the surprise in his eyes and I grinned back at him and leaned in and kissed him. His lips were sweet and firm, and I felt a slight shock run through me as our lips met. He pulled back from me slightly with an awe-struck look on his face.

"Wow, Lexi. Just wow."

"What did you think?" I asked, shyly.

"I think that's the kiss I've been waiting for my whole life." Luke shook his head as if he couldn't quite believe what had happened. "I don't really know what to say."

"I think right now you should be quiet." I put my finger to his lips. "I want to talk to you."
"I won't say no to that." He bit the tip of my finger and I squealed.
"Luke!"
"Sorry." He laughed, looking like he wasn't sorry at all. "Where should we go to talk?"
"We can go to my room…"
"Are your parents home?" I made a face.
"No. They went to Minneapolis to visit my aunt."
"Then let's go to your room." I grabbed his hand and we walked into his house.
"Do you want anything to drink or eat?"
"Luke! No," I laughed. "Please. I just need to talk to you."
"Okay okay." He grinned and we ran up the stairs. I jumped onto his bed and lay down as soon as we walked in and he lay down next to me. "So, you wanted to tell me something?"
I rolled over and looked at his earnest and trusting eyes and I was reminded of how I nearly lost this wonderful man. "I did." I took a deep breath and Luke leaned in and kissed me. This time he was the aggressor and his tongue plunged into my mouth, tantalizing me with its strokes. I felt warmness in my belly and pressed myself closer to him, wanting to feel him closer to me. I reached my hands up to his head and ran my fingers through it, loving the feel of him on my fingertips.
Luke groaned and pulled away from me. "Sorry. I shouldn't have done that."
"I'm glad you did," I sighed.
"But don't you want to talk to me first?"
"I guess," I moaned and licked my lips. Luke's eyes fell to my lips and I could see a tremble in his throat.

"Don't lick your lips if you want me to keep my hands off of you."

"Who says I want you to keep your hands off of me?"

"I want to hear what you came to say." Luke's voice was low and I think I saw a flush rising up from his neck. Luke was nervous. I grabbed his hands and I held them close to my heart.

"Luke. When I was in school I took a philosophy class. And in that class we all discussed a story."

"Okay." He looked confused. Maybe because he knew I didn't really like philosophy.

"Basically, this story talked about this village. It was the happiest village in the world. Everyone who lived there was happy and rich and everything in their life was perfect. The only problem was, for everyone to be happy, there was one young boy tied up in a cellar at the edge of the town. He was trapped in a little basement and tied with chains. He only had water to drink and dry bread to eat and his life was miserable. And he had to stay locked up. Because, if he was let loose, the village would become normal. Meaning that there would be misery, anger and poverty. So, for the sake of the village, that one kid had to suffer."

"That's horrible." Luke frowned.

"It is horrible," I agreed. "Anyways, in class we all discussed what we thought should happen, should they let him loose, should he stay tied up?"

"He should be let loose."

"I agree." I smiled at him, briefly. "No one should be sacrificed so that someone else can be happy."

"Good." He looked at me curiously. "Why did you tell me this story?" He cocked his head and laughed. "You're not about to tell me that you would be that boy for me, are you?"

I gazed into his eyes and a single tear rolled down my cheek. "No. But you would be that boy for me. You've already been that boy for me."
"I'm not…" He shook his head and I reached over and kept it still. I leaned towards him and stared into his eyes.
"Luke, you have put my feelings before you in everything that you have ever done. And I always took you for granted. I nearly lost you. I hope I haven't lost you." I stared into his eyes, searching for an answer and he shook his head silently.
"You know, in fairytales, there is one great love for the princess. Her Prince Charming is always the one and they ride off into the sunset and her old life is left behind. But what they don't tell you is that the Prince isn't always the one. Sometimes it's the faithful farm boy who's always been by her side, through thick and thin. Sometimes a princess doesn't need a prince."
"Are you saying I'm not a Prince?" He smiled, slowly.
"I'm saying you're better than a Prince. I'm saying you're my best friend, my everything. You've been the sunshine sitting in my pocket while I've been waiting for the rain to stop."
"I like being the sunshine in your pocket."
"I like you liking that."
"I like you liking me like that."
"I like that you're a goof." I laughed and he leaned over and kissed my nose.
"I like that I can lean over and kiss your nose now."
"You always kiss my nose."
"But I didn't do this afterwards." Luke reached over to kiss me and rolled me over so that he was lying on top of me. His arms were splayed to the side of me so that he wasn't resting all of his weight on me. He leaned down and kissed

me again and, this time, he rested his chest against me. I put my arms around him and he played with my hair as he kissed me. His lips left my mine and trailed down my neck. I felt his tongue against my skin and I squirmed against him.
"Luke," I giggled, feeling somewhat uncomfortable, but extremely happy.
"Yes, my love."
I don't know..." My words cut off as I felt his tongue run over my breast. Even though I still had on my top and bra, I felt the tip of his tongue against me. "Oh Luke."
"Can I take off your top, Lexi?" He looked into my eyes again and I nodded. He pulled my top off and I lifted my arms up so he could get it all the way off. "You're beautiful, Lexi."
"Ssh," I laughed, shaking my head.
"Your breasts fit the palms of my hands perfectly." He grinned as he cupped my breasts through the bra. His finger slipped up into my bra and I squealed as he pinched me.
"What are you doing?" I breathed in shock, barely believing he had just touched me there.
"Do you trust me, Lexi?"
"With my life," I nodded.
"Do you love me?" He whispered, hopefully. He was on top of me, looking into my eyes, keenly, with a scared concern on his face.
"I love you with all my heart and soul, Luke Bryan."
"Oh Lexi." He burst into a huge grin and showered kisses all over my chest. "You don't know how I've longed to hear you say those words."
"Oh you have, have you?"
"Yes." He leaned down and stroked the hair away from my face. "I want you to know something."

"Uh oh," I groaned. "I'm scared."
"Don't be," he sighed. "I need you to know something."
"What? You're killing me here, Luke."
"I never slept with Briget," he mumbled.
"What?" I frowned. "You what?"
"I never slept with Briget."
"But I always saw you guys kissing and stuff."
"Well, yeah we kissed," he laughed. "But we never had sex."
"Why not?"
"I was hoping you'd come around." He blushed.
"What!" I screamed and pushed him off of me. "Are you joking?" I was now sitting on top of him.
"No. I just wanted you to be my first."
"Luke!"
"I mean, it's not like we didn't do stuff. We got naked and fooled around but…"
I groaned. "I don't want to hear about you and Briget. Yuck."
"Oh, Lexi." He laughed.
"I can't believe you're a virgin."
"Do you remember when we were sixteen and you said that you thought it would be the most romantic thing in the world for two people in love to be each other's firsts?"
"I was sixteen, Luke," I sighed. "I can't believe this."
"Are you upset?" He frowned at me. "I'm pretty sure I can still pleasure you, Lexi. I have developed my skills and seen enough movies."
"Are you talking about pornos, Luke?" I laughed. "Those are not movies."
"They're sex movies." He laughed and he adjusted his body.
"Luke," I squealed and moaned slightly as I felt him move

under me.
"What?" He held my hips and stared up at me. "I like you sitting here like this, Lexi."
"I'm sure you do." I laughed and then bit my lip. "There's something else I need to tell you, Luke."
"Go on."
"It's about what you just told me and Bryce…" I mumbled, looking away from him, embarrassed.
"It's okay Lexi." He grabbed my face and turned it to face his. "Look at me, Lexi."
I turned my face towards his and his eyes were shining with unshed tears. "Lexi, I don't care what you did with Bryce, or with any other guy for that matter. Your past doesn't make a difference to me. You're still my Lexi, my sweet, beautiful, wonderful Lexi."
"I thought we were meant to be—"
"—Ssh." He brought me down towards him. "I know how you felt about Bryce, Lexi. Hell, even I can tell he's hot. And he's a broken soul. I know how much you like to fix broken souls. But you chose me. And that's all I care about."
"I don't deserve you, Luke."
"Lexi, do you know how much I love you?"
I shake my head and hide a smile.
"Let me count the ways." I felt his fingers on my bra straps and as he pulled them down I giggled. I heard him unclasping the hook before I felt it being undone and I fell forward, laughing, as he threw my bra across the room.
"Touchdown!" He shouted and kissed me.
"Take your shirt off." I laughed and pull his shirt up. His chest is more defined than I remember it being and I ran my hands across his stomach and pecks, laughing as he twitched his muscles beneath my fingers. "You're

beautiful." I kissed his chest and down his happy trail until I'm at his pants. I looked up and he grinned down at me and then I kissed all the way back up to his lips. "You wish, Luke Bryan."

"You know me soo well." He winked at me and rolled me over onto my back. This time it is his turn to kiss me and I felt his lips all over my face and neck. I closed my eyes and clutched the sheets as I felt his lips on my breasts. Then he started nibbling on my peaks with his teeth and I groaned. I heard his laughter as he continued kissing down my stomach to the top of my pants. Only he's braver than I and I felt him unzip my pants and then he pulled them down. I was lying on his bed, almost naked, and all I could think about was, why did I wait so long for this to happen? My body felt like it was fire and I felt a deep, wanton urge awaken inside of me. I wanted to make love to Luke. I wanted him to make love to me and devour me. And I wanted us to merge our bodies together so that no one could ever part us.

I finally opened my eyes and looked up to see Luke pulling down his boxer trunks. I looked away, quickly, not wanting to be caught staring at his manhood. I quickly looked back to take a look. I can't not look at his magnificent body. He caught me staring at him and grinned, before crawling back onto the bed to join me. His member brushed across my leg and I gasped.

"Don't you want me to be naked as well?" I whispered.

"If that's what you want."

"Of course I want." I smiled. "Do you have protection?"

"Yes." He grinned and I noticed that he had some packets in his hand. "They were in my wallet."

"I'm not even going to ask why."

"Okay." He just stood there; so I pulled him down to join

me on the bed.
"What are you waiting on, Luke?" I whispered in his ear and he started to tickle me. We rolled around on the bed and I suddenly realized that he was on top of me, his pelvic bone was crushed into me, and his manhood was pressed up against my most intimate of places. I then realized that I don't want to wait any longer. I need to feel all of him.
He seemed to sense what I was feeling, because, before I knew it, he had pulled my underwear down with his teeth and he grabbed the packet next to the bed and ripped it open. I watched as he slid it on quickly and smoothly and then I felt him inside of me and I felt like I had somehow died and gone to heaven. It was the most exquisite and sweetest feeling I've ever felt in my life and I felt like every nerve end in my body was celebrating our union.
I held onto him tightly and I heard voices groaning and moaning. I felt bodies writhing and moving. And it felt like an out of body experience. I felt like I was floating on air. Everything about our lovemaking was magical and I was the recipient of the most intense pleasure in the world. And then I got to the top of the rollercoaster and I was falling, screaming, crying out in excitement and pleasure. I felt Luke's lips on mine, kissing me urgently and, as he collapsed onto me, heaving and grunting, I held him close and smiled.
I'd been in Luke's bed many, many times, but never had we had an experience like this. This was an experience I could have once in my life and be satisfied forever. This was what making love was all about. For a fleeting moment, I thought about my experience with Bryce and I felt a pang of shame and distress. My union with Bryce had been nothing like this. I had given my virginity to him and the experience had meant nothing. I wanted to feel sorry for myself but I

didn't. In a way, I was thankful that I had had that experience, so I could appreciate even more what it was like to make love to a man I truly loved as opposed to a man I had lusted after. But still I felt guilty.

I knew that Bryce was heartbroken over his mother's death and that he felt bad over cheating on me. I knew internally that that was his bad, but I still felt like I should have spoken to him before I came to Luke's.

"Are you okay, Lexi?" Luke looked at me with concern. "Did I hurt you?"

"I'm fine, my love." I kissed him and smiled. "That was amazing."

"I thought so as well." He grinned. "And to think that was my first time, I'll be a regular Don Juan in a few weeks."

"You better not turn into a Don Juan," I laughed.

"Are you really okay?" He studied my face and I pulled him down to me.

"I'm fine." I snuggled into his arms and closed my eyes. "This is, most probably, the best I had ever felt in my life."

"I think I have to admit this beat out the day I found out MIT was offering me a full scholarship." He laughed and played with my hair as I lay in his arms. I could feel him growing against my thigh again and I grinned.

"Well I'm glad to hear I beat out MIT." I laughed and giggled as Luke tickled me in places he never had before. I turned around to face him and delighted in this next step of our relationship, but my mind was left wondering what would happen next. Now that he had brought up MIT I wanted to know if he was still going to move to Boston and if he was, what would it mean for us?

Before I had a chance to ask Luke what would come next, he kissed his way down to my womanhood and I closed my eyes as I felt him down there and he took me to places I never knew existed before.

Chapter 6
Bryce

I picked up a Barbie from the local toy store to take Shelby. I wasn't sure if she would like it, but I figured I had pretty good odds. What little girl didn't like dolls? I still had some time to kill after I left the store, so I decided to go and get her some flowers as well. I settled on sunflowers instead of roses. Roses seemed too grown up for a little kid. I wanted to get her sunflowers because I wanted her to know that she was like sunshine in my life. I figured she was too young to understand the symbolism, but I figured she would appreciate it when I explained it to her when she was older. I thought about picking some flowers up for Lexi as well, but I hadn't heard back from her after I had tried calling her back the day before. I figured she must be angry at me for what had happened with Anna. I hadn't minded that she hadn't called me back. I didn't deserve it. And I wasn't really ready to talk. Not yet. It was a big move to ask her to marry me. I wanted to make sure that I was ready. Really ready. And I honestly didn't know if I was.

All I could think about was my mom and what she had been through. I wondered what would have happened if I hadn't joined the marines. Maybe she would have left my dad earlier and then she'd still be alive. I tried not to let those thoughts burn and fester in my mind. I knew it wasn't helpful. That's what the doctor had told me. *Don't dwell on the negative, Bryce; it will only bring you down.* And I tried now, more than ever, to remember what he said and to live by it. I couldn't depend on the pills anymore.

My father told me that the funeral was going to be in a few days. I didn't quite get it. How could it take nine months for a baby to come into the world but only a few days to bury someone once they died? I didn't want to have to say that final goodbye. The previous night, when I was sleeping in my bed, I kept waiting to hear my mother's footsteps as she went back and forth doing her daily chores. I was waiting to hear her singing in the shower like she always did. But all that greeted me was silence.

My father and I didn't talk, save for him telling me about the funeral. I had nothing to say to him. And it seemed that he had nothing to say to me either. I couldn't tell if he was upset or not. He was so hard to read these days.

"Hey, Bryce, sorry I'm late." Luke ran up to me and joined me in the hospital lobby with a huge smile on his face.

"No worries, I just got here." I nodded and held up the Barbie. "I stopped to get Shelby a present. I hope it's okay."

"She'll love it." He grinned and flashed a badge to the nurse behind the desk. "Let's go up."

"It's okay for me to visit her?"

"Yeah." He nodded. "Now she's in remission, we don't have to take any special precautions. And she loves visitors, so she'll be happy to see you."

"I wish Lexi could have come as well." I sighed. "But she's not talking to me right now."

"Oh?" He looked at me quickly and turned away with a slight flush on his face. I'm sure he felt bad for me after everything that had happened.

"I think she must be mad because of Anna."

"I guess so." He nodded.

"She did call and leave me a message yesterday, though." I paused. "I'm sure she must be unsure of what to do, what with my mom dying and me dropping this bombshell on the same day."

"Yeah."

"Sorry, I'm sure you don't want to hear about it."
"I don't know what to say." He looked at me with worried eyes. "I hope you guys get to talk soon."
"I've been thinking about proposing to her." I laughed at his shocked expression. "I know it's fast, but it just seems so right, you know. She's loved me for years, and well I want her to know that I appreciate her faith in me. I just can't believe I never really noticed her in high school."
"Yeah, I don't know how anyone can pass over Lexi Lord."
"Sorry, man." I cringed as I thought about whom I was gushing to. He most probably thought I was throwing our relationship in his face. I was pretty sure he was in love with her as well. C'mon Bryce, I thought to myself. Be a gentleman. "Anyways, I'm excited to see Shelby."
"Do you want to tell her you're her brother?"
"I can do that?" I was surprised.
"Well, if you don't plan on visiting her often, then I wouldn't recommend it." He looked at me curiously. "So I guess I'm asking is this going to be a one visit type of thing?"
"But she won't be in the hospital much longer will she? If she's in remission."
"No, she'll be going back to the orphanage. But you can still visit her then. Maybe even take her out for an afternoon."
"Oh, I don't know if I can do that." I felt panicked. "I don't know anything about little kids."
"It's not too hard."
"But she's a girl as well. I don't know anything about little girls." My hands clammed up and I stopped. "Maybe I shouldn't visit her. Will you give her the Barbie instead?"
"Hey Bryce." Luke put his hand on my shoulder. "It'll be okay. I promise. Just come and meet her properly. You can

decide what you're comfortable with."
"Okay." I took a deep breath. "Okay, I'm ready."
Luke pushed the door open and Shelby ran towards him as I just stood there like a statue. "Lukey." I watched as he picked her up and swung her around. I saw her blue eyes sparkling with happiness. She smiled as she saw me and waved energetically.
"Hiya." I waved back at her and plastered a big smile on my face.
"Hi, I member you from yesterday." She walked over to me as Luke put her down and I put my hand out for her to shake.
"I thought I'd come and say hello." I smiled, gently, and handed her the Barbie. "I bought this for you to play with."
Shelby took the Barbie from me and held it in her hands like a sacred object. "For me?" She looked surprised and I nodded.
"Yes, for you."
"Thank you." She leaned over to give me a hug and I held her tightly.
"You're welcome."
"I'm Shelby."
"I'm Bryce."
"I like the name Bryce." She giggled and I am reminded of Lexi. She had Lexi's smile I thought to myself. *That's why she seems so familiar.*
"And I like the name Shelby."
"We both have blue eyes." She pointed at me.
"Yes we do." And I felt as if I'd been shot. She had my eyes. I looked into her face and I saw my reflection shining back at me through her sky blue irises. She had my eyes and she had Lexi's smile. In a weird way, she could have been the image of what a kid of mine and Lexi's would

look like.
"Want to play top chef?"
"What's that?"
"We pretend to cook stuff. Lukey, you be the judge."
"Okay, Shelby." He grinned at her. "I like your bandana today." He pointed at the pink piece of fabric on her head and she twirled around.
"It's 'cos I'm a princess," she giggled.
"Princess Shelby is a fine name." Luke teased her and she turned towards me.
"Do you like it Brycey?"
"I love it." A warm feeling enveloped me and I bowed down in front of her. "I am at your service, Princess Shelby."
"You can be King Brycey and you can be Prince Lukey." She ran to the corner of her room and picked up a red teddy bear. "And this is going to be the wicked witch." She threw him across the room and ran towards me. "Save me from the witch, King Brycey, save me from the witch."
I laughed and grabbed her and held her in the air. "I have you safe Princess."
"You saved me. You're my King." She giggled and planted a soft kiss on my cheek. I put her back down on the ground and Luke pointed at her with a mock stern look. "I thought we were playing top chef?"
"We can play that next time." She giggled and took my hand. "Come and see my picture." I walked with her to the bed and she picked up a piece of paper with a drawing.
"What's this?" I smiled at her. "Are you a top artist as well?"
She nodded her head and smiled. "This is my new family. Now I'm all better, I can get a mom and a dad and a big dog."

"Oh?" I tried to keep the smile on my face, but I felt like my insides were being torn to shreds.
"A family will want me now because I'm a princess and I'm all well." She grinned and I saw that her front tooth was missing. I wanted to pull her into my arms and never let her go. A child that small shouldn't be worried about things like families, I thought with a sigh. I looked at Luke and he gave me a half smile, I could see the stress and concern in his eyes as well.
"Anybody would be happy to have a princess like you as their daughter." I stroked her head and she yawned.
"I'm just going to relax my eyes for a few seconds. Don't go. I want to play still, okay?" She looked up at me with a hopeful expression, her bandana had slipped off and I saw the beginnings of hair growth on her scalp.
"Of course."
"Good." She lay back and held my hand. "Then after my quick rest we can play Superman."
"Okay." I watched as she drifted to sleep and I felt my heartbeat start to slow down.
"Come." Luke ushered me towards the door. "Let's go get a coffee."
"But I promised her I'll stay." I frowned and don't move.
"She'll be asleep for a while. She's exhausted from the excitement. We'll come back."
"Okay." I frowned and followed him out the door. "Does she always get tired so quickly?"
"She's getting better," Luke grinned. "Sometimes she would fall asleep in midsentence."
"Oh." I was glad that I had missed out on witnessing her go through chemotherapy. I wasn't sure if I would have been strong enough to keep her together. "So, what happens to her now…" My voice drifted off.

"Now your mom can't adopt her?" Luke finished for me and I nodded. I studied his face and I could see why he was such an important person in Lexi's life. He was a good guy. I didn't feel jealous of him anymore. How could I? He was my little sister's best friend. "Well, hopefully another family will adopt her."

"Someone in Jonesville?"

"Maybe. Or even someone from Illinois or even Missouri. We have a lot of families looking for children. They don't all need to stay in the State. Shelby can go anywhere. Full rights to her were given up."

"But she can't leave Jonesville. How will we see her?" My voice rose with panic. "I just met her, she can't leave."

"It's not going to happen overnight, Bryce." Luke put his hand on my shoulder again. "You'll figure out a way to stay in touch."

"I want her to know." I said the words before I even thought about them properly. "I want her to know I'm her brother."

"What about Lexi?"

"She can decide for herself." I sighed. "But I want Shelby to know today."

"Don't you want to discuss it with Lexi first? See what she wants to do as well?"

"No." My answer was firm. I didn't know what was going to happen with Lexi, or when. I wanted her to get to know Shelby as well, but I wasn't going to delay telling her the truth because of that. Lexi had known about Shelby her whole life and she had never told me. I didn't owe her this now. I hardened my heart to the slight guilt I felt. I loved Lexi, but I wasn't going to let that love take over everything in my life. "I'd like to tell her when we go back in the room."

"Okay then." Luke frowned but he didn't say anything else to me.
"Don't judge me, Luke. You haven't told her about Shelby either."
"I know." He looked away. "I hope it wasn't a mistake."
"She's a special girl."
"Yes." I heard the smile in his voice and I felt like an asshole for bringing her up.
"I'm sorry by the way." I spoke quickly, knowing I had to say something.
"For?"
"Having her heart."
"Oh."
"Shall we see if Shelby's up?" I changed the subject, not wanting to continue the conversation.
"Let me make a call first." I watched as Luke walked away and I took a seat. My head was pounding but, this time, I wasn't upset or worried. I was just excited and happy to be alive. I wanted to make my mom proud. I wanted to do something that would make everything worth it. I wanted to be the man that she knew I could be. At twenty-three, I wasn't much of a man. Yes, the marines had shaped me, strengthened me in some ways, but, ultimately, I'd always hidden behind my façade. I had always told myself that I was a failure, that my whole life was a lie, that I was never the golden boy and could never be. Part of me had rebelled from that label for as long as I could remember. I didn't think I fit the title and I didn't think I ever could. But what struck me most, was that I never even tried. I was always defeated before I started. I was always running away from the truth, unable to face up to the pain and stress I felt at not being good enough.
My heart jumped as my phone rang and I looked down at it,

eagerly, hoping it was Lexi. I sighed as I saw that it was Anna. I was about to put the phone back in my pocket, unanswered, but decided to answer it. I had treated her badly. In fact, she was most probably the one who was affected the most by what I had said.
"Hi, Anna."
"Bryce." Her voice was soft, unsure and I felt a sudden overwhelming urge to hug her.
"Are you okay?" I said, gruffly. "I'm sorry I told Lexi."
"Don't apologize, Bryce," she sighed. "What I did was wrong. I'm glad you told her. It allowed me to air many problems that had been plaguing our friendship."
"Oh man, I hope you guys are okay."
"I'm not sure if we'll ever be okay, but that's okay." She cleared her throat and continued. "I was actually calling to see if you're okay."
"Me?" I was surprised that she had called after everything that had happened. "I can't lie, it hurts like hell, but I'm trying to just get through each day as best as I can."
"My mom died when I was young. I know what it's like to lose a parent you love." Her voice was soothing to the ear and I leaned back against the wall and closed my eyes and listened. "My words and words from others won't even patch the pain, but I want you to know I'm here if you ever need me, to talk or whatever."
"Thank you, Anna."
"I know that may be hard because of what happened and Lexi and stuff, but I'm here if you ever feel lonely." She paused and I had the feeling that she was crying.
"What are you doing this afternoon?" I asked her, against my better judgment.
"Nothing, why?" She sounded surprised.
"I was thinking maybe we could hang out, go somewhere

and talk."
"Are you sure?"
"Yeah. I'm sure." It seemed to me that Anna needed it more than I did.
"Thanks, do you mind…"
"Picking you up?" I laughed. "Not at all. I'll text you when I'm on the way."
As I hung up, I saw Luke in front of me with a curious look on his face, "Who was that?"
"Uh, Lexi," I lied, for some reason not wanting him to know that I was going to meet Anna.
"Oh? You guys are going to meet up?"
"Yeah. After I leave here."
"Huh, okay." He looked unhappy and my heart went out to him. What a horrible situation for us all to be in.
"Shall we go and see Shelby again?"
"I'm afraid the doctor has asked if we wait until another day to give her the news. He doesn't want to overwhelm her."
"Sure that makes sense." I tried to hide my disappointment. I had wanted Shelby to know now. I had wanted her to know she had a family. A brother who was here to love and spoil her.
"You should decide what you're going to tell your dad, if you decide to make this public." Luke's voice was low and I could see the concern on his face. He was right. I hadn't even thought about what my dad would say if it got out that I was spending time with my little sister. Everyone would know what a fake he was then. I frowned while thinking. I couldn't let it get out about Shelby or my dad would do whatever it took to discredit me and keep us apart.
"Luke, I'm going to ask you to keep this quiet."
"What?"

"If my dad finds out about Shelby, he's going to ship her off somewhere as fast as he can. He is not going to want this to get out."
"I can see that. I won't tell anyone."
"We can't tell Lexi either."
"I don't know if I'm comfortable with that, Bryce." Luke rubbed his temple. "I think Lexi has a right to know."
"Of course she does, but not right now." I looked at him earnestly. "We can't let her know right now. It could spoil everything."
"Spoil what?"
"I have a plan." I spoke slowly, my mind racing a hundred miles a minute. "But I'm not going to tell you. I have to work on this by myself. I just need some time."
"I don't know, Bryce."
"Please, Luke. Please do this for me. You've kept it a secret from Lexi for this long already, what's another few weeks?"
"But this is different now."
"What's different?" I lean in towards him. "What's different now, Luke?"
He turned his face away from me and sighed. "It's not my place to say anything."
"Good." I nodded my head.
"I didn't mean about Shelby…" His voice faded and he shook his head. "Okay, Bryce, I'll keep my mouth shut for now. For you and for your mother."
"Thanks." I reached over and shook his hand. "You're a good guy, Luke."
"I'll see you tomorrow?"
"No. I've got to see a man about a dog. But I'll call you when I have some news."
"Okay. Well have a good time with Lexi." His voice

sounded distraught and I ignored the urge to pull him close to me.

“I … I will.” I frowned and turned away, already disgusted with the lie. “See-ya.” I looked at my watch and decided to make a quick trip into town before I went to go and see Anna. There was someone I needed to speak to urgently. I had to make a visit to Mr. Raynor. He was my mom’s lawyer, the one who was filing for her divorce. I only hoped that he still had the paperwork I needed to see.

Chapter 7
Lexi

"Should I call him?" I played with my hair as Luke sat next to me on the bed.
"No, I wouldn't call him now." He kissed my neck and I snuggled into him, breathing in his cologne and manly essence.
"I do want him to know I'm here for him, you know." I sighed. "Where did you say you saw him again?"
"At the store. He was getting something to eat."
"And he told you he was on his way to meet me?"
"Yeah, something like that." He sighed. "He's obviously not in a good place right now."
"Maybe I should go and visit him. Explain that I still care about him."
"You may just hurt him even more, Lexi."
"I don't want to hurt him," I sighed. "I just don't want him to grieve alone."
"I don't know if you can just be his friend at this point, Lexi. He is convinced it is a lot more than that."
"I thought it was," I moaned. "I thought we were meant to be. I made a mistake."
"You can't tell him that now."
"Maybe he would understand. He knows I never really knew him. My crush was just a fantasy that built and built. I allowed it to go too far."
"Lexi, you know I love you. But this is not the time to tell a guy whose mother has just died that your love for him was a figment of your imagination."
"You don't think I should be honest?"
"I think you should just let it go for now." His hand reached under my tee shirt and he started nibbling on my lips. "His

heart has just been broken. Don't break it again."
"Oh Luke." I grabbed his head and looked into his eyes. "How did I get so lucky to get you?"
"Your mom bought the right house."
"Yeah." I laughed. "She did something right."
"You know Lexi, love isn't always what we expect it to be." Luke pulled away from me and he ran his fingers over my eyebrows, smoothly them down gently. "Sometimes love is knowing when to let something go, or knowing when to keep something to oneself."
"But lies never help."
"Give him some time, Lexi. He has a lot going on."
"Since when have you been on his side?"
"I'm not taking sides. I'm just saying that maybe everything is too black and white for you. That rarely works in life. You don't just love one person and hate another. You don't just fall in love in a day and you don't fall in love in one day either. Emotions are complicated. The truth is complicated. Sometimes that grey area is where things need to be."
"I don't want to be in that grey area. Not anymore."
"Lexi, last week you were overjoyed that Bryce was back in town and was inviting you to his party. Last night you were in my bed, telling me how much you love me. Forgive me when I say this, my dear, but you are the grey area."
I pulled away from him and jumped out of the bed, hurt. "How could you say that to me Luke? Do you think I'm some sort of slut?"
He sighed deeply and stood up. "I'm not saying that, Lexi. I know you inside and out. I love who you are. But everything's going so fast in your mind. In fact, I don't even know what's going on in your mind."
"What do you mean?"

"Yesterday I told you I loved you and you panicked. The next thing I know you're in my bed, telling me you love me too. I want to know what caused the change."
"I realized that I loved you," I mumbled, upset.
"How?"
"A butterfly told me."
"What?"
"Nothing." I pulled on my pants and I pushed past him. "I can't believe we're doing this now."
"Why, Lexi?" He grabbed a hold of my arm. "Why can't we have this conversation? How did you go from Bryce being the love your life to me in less than a week?"
"Do you want me to be with Bryce, Luke?" I turned around and shouted. "Is that what you want? He cheated on me, Luke, do you want me to be with a cheater?"
"If he hadn't cheated on you, would you be here right now, Lexi?" His tone was soft, silky, and smooth. It was only his eyes that belied the importance of this question to him.
"I don't know," I whispered softly. "I don't know."
"So there you have it," he laughed roughly. "I'm really your second best."
"No Luke, you're not. You don't understand," I cried out, trying to get him to understand. "Yes, I thought I loved Bryce. I've been infatuated with him since high school but I don't really know him. I was in love with a dream. You are the guy for me, Luke. You are better than my dreams. I just didn't realize it."
"But you realize it now Bryce cheated on you?"
"Yes. No. I mean, that's not what I mean. His cheating made me really examine my feelings and what I wanted out of life. Who I wanted."
"Forgive me, Lexi, but it still makes me feel like second best."

"You told me you weren't upset," I shouted at him. "You told me you didn't care that I had slept with Bryce."
"It's not about you fucking him, Lexi. It's about us. Why can't there be an explanation for an us that doesn't involve him?"
"Luke, please." I felt the tears running down my face, and my breath came in little spurts. These are the ugly sort of tears, the ones that give you splotchy marks and weird breathing. The kind that you don't want others to see.
"What do you want me to say, Lexi?" He shook his head. "I can't make your guilt and your pain go away. And neither can Bryce. None of us can fix you, Lexi. We can cover a hole, but eventually that cover is going to fall off. You have to fix yourself."
"I don't need fixing!" I screamed. "I'm perfectly fine." I fell to his bed, sobbing into the sheets.
"No, Lexi. No you're not." He sat next to me and rubbed my back. "Maybe that's why you and Bryce were both drawn to each other. You both have scars deeper than the eyes sight. But you're going about it wrong. No one else can heal those scars, Lexi, only you can."
I turned around slowly then and looked at him through tear-drenched eyes. "That's where you're wrong, Luke. Love can heal all scars."
"That's a fairytale, Lexi. Why can't you grow up? Love can't fix everything. No one is perfect."
"No one is perfect, Luke but I'm not looking for perfection. I love you because of everything you are. Who you are. I've always loved you. It just took a kick in the head to show me."
"Lexi, I'm sorry. I didn't mean to upset you." He looked worried and I leaned over and kissed him.
"You don't get it, do you, Luke? You're not the problem.

You will never be the problem.” I laughed through my tears. “Though that may not always be true. I’ve got some issues. I know that. I’ve never really gotten over some things related to my dad, but I don’t need to hide in my daydreams any more. You’re the most honest, wonderful human being I’ve ever met in my life and you are always here for me. You say love can’t fix everything, but I’m here to tell you that that’s not true. Your love has healed me. It has helped me to be confident and true to myself. My journey’s not over. No, it’s just beginning. But I am confident that I can complete it because I have you in my life.”

“You must really love me.” He half smiled and I hit him in the arm.

“You’re a goof, Luke Bryan.”

“Do you love me enough to watch ‘Madea Goes to Jail’ right now?”

“Are you joking me?” I laugh. “You are the only white guy, no scratch that, the only guy in the world who wants to watch Madea.”

“She’s funny,” he laughs. “And if you pay attention, she has a lot of good wisdom.”

“I’m not getting my wisdom from a man dressed as a woman.”

“But you will from a butterfly?” He cocked his head and I pushed him onto the bed before slowly getting on top of him.

“I’ll have you know that butterflies say the most incredible things.”

“Like?”

“Well,” I grinned at him and unbuckled his jeans. “I can’t do two things at once.”

“Lexi, you know that I’m always here for you right? You

don't have to ever hide anything from me."
"I know and I feel the same." I pulled his pants down and I see that he is ready for what I have planned.
"I want you to know that I understand if there are things you can't tell me." He gasped as I pulled his boxers down and took him in my hands.
"What was that?"
"Nothing." He grunts and lies back, allowing me to pleasure him in a way I had never known I would enjoy so much before.

***

Sex makes you sleepy. I know, I know, that's something I should have known from the movies or something. But as I stretched and reached out for Luke, I realized that he wasn't in the bed. I heard him whispering and I lay still, trying to hear what he was saying.
"Hey, yeah I saw Bryce at the hospital," he sighed. "I see. Yeah, I thought he might be trying to plan something like that. You didn't tell him anything, did you?" I saw him peak around the room and I closed my eyes quickly. "I don't want anyone to know. I can't do that, you know that. I think you should move forward. Okay. I'll come to see you next week." He hung up the phone quickly as my mind was scrambling. Why had he said that he had seen Bryce at the hospital? I thought he had seen him at a café or shop? Why would he lie to me?
I felt my heart beating fast and I turned over as I felt him get into bed with me. He curled up next to me and I felt his arm come around my waist to fondle my breast. He moved up against me and spooned me and my body betrayed me by pushing back into him. I lay in his arms, wondering if I

truly knew who he was. Who had he been talking to?
I must have fallen asleep again, because I woke up a few hours later to the sounds of the TV.
"Hey, sleepyhead." Luke grinned at me. "Did I wake you up?"
"No," I yawned.
"What do you want to do?"
"I think I should go home." I averted my eyes and slid out of the bed. "My mom's most probably wondering where I am."
"Can't you stay?"
"I stayed over last night." I pulled on my tee shirt quickly and he held up my bra.
"Going braless?" He licked his lips.
"Well I'm just going next door."
"You can go braless with me at any time." He jumped up and pulled me towards him.
"I'll see you later." I rushed out of the door and Luke followed me down the stairs.
"Lexi, wait a sec."
I turned around and he kissed me. I melted against him and kissed him back, trying to fight back tears.
"You know I love you right, Lexi?" He took my hands into his and rubbed them. The friction created a warm glow in me and I nodded my head. "There is nothing I wouldn't do to make you happy."
"You're lucky you know, Luke." I looked around us. "Even though your parents aren't rich with money, you've always had such a great upbringing, such a great happy family."
"I know. I've been very lucky to have gotten the parents that I did. Others aren't always so lucky."
"Yeah, some people just shouldn't be parents."
"Lexi, I want you to know I'm not going to go to Boston."

“But what about MIT?” I frowned as he changed the subject.
“I’m not going to go. I don’t need the degree. I’m doing fine.”
“But you’ve been so excited, Luke.”
“I don’t want to leave you here.”
“I can come with you.” I bit my lip and he shook his head.
“That’s not your dream, Lexi. I can’t make you go to Boston.”
“You can’t not go, Luke.”
“We can talk about it later, okay?”
“Fine.” I sighed. “We’ll work it out, but one thing I ask, Luke, is please never lie to me.” I leaned over and kissed him before I turned to leave. “Please never lie to me.”
I walked out of the front door and I saw him standing there, watching me. He watched me with caged eyes and, as I waved at him, I realized that he had been right about one thing. The hole in my heart was still there. Our love hadn’t fixed the emptiness inside. It had only covered it up and now I wasn’t sure if I had made the right decision. I knew that I loved Luke, but at least Bryce had told me the truth about him and Anna.

Chapter 8
Bryce

"I really wanted to adopt Bongo myself, but my dad said no more dogs." Anna laughed as she told me stories about her pets and I smiled back at her eager look. It was refreshing to be with someone who had no agenda and was open and honest.
"Bongo sounds like a handful." I cleared my throat and coughed after I spoke.
"I'm sorry." She cleared her throat, nervously. "I didn't mean to bore you."
"You're not boring me." I took her hand and squeezed it. "In fact, I appreciate you spending the evening with me."
"You're easy to talk to. Like Eddie was." She looked up at me with wide, innocent eyes. "He was a cool guy. You know, he always used to call me the prettiest tutor in the world."
"You really miss Eddie, don't you?"
"No one ever called me pretty before." She stared at her fingers, blushing. "Not that I expect it or anything. I know I'm a bit of a plain Jane."
"But you're gorgeous." I protested quickly.
Anna laughed and flicked her hair back. "You don't have to lie. I know I'm a bit of a wallflower. But he really made me feel pretty."
My heart broke for her as she spoke. I'd never seen anyone with that little self-confidence before. Maybe she needed to trade a little with Suzannah, who had an over abundance of confidence.
"You're a good guy, Bryce. I never really saw what Lexi saw in you in high school, but I think I get it now."
"You think so?" I grinned and she laughed.

"Well you know." She shrugged. "You were always such a jerk. It was like you thought you were King of the school."
"Well break it to me easy, why don't cha?"
"Sorry. I'm not one to mince my words." She laughed. "I supported Lexi and her crush, though. I wasn't really worried because I never thought you'd be interested in her."
"She's really liked me a long time, huh?"
"Yeah." She nodded her head, despondently. "I can't believe I did that to her."
"Hey," I grabbed her hands. "It took two to tango."
"I guess." She looked away and I felt awful for making her feel bad.
"Do you want another milkshake?" I slurped up the rest of my strawberry shake and she laughed.
"With some chili cheese fries?"
"You like chili cheese fries?" My mouth fell open.
"With lots of onions on them!" She laughed. "I'm not the sort of girl who worries about her breath."
"That wasn't what I meant."
"Farts?" She looked puzzled and I laughed even harder.
"No. I meant most girls are watching their figures."
"Oh." She joined in with my laughter. "I'm not worried about it."
"I can see why." I looked her up and down and admired her figure. I wanted to kick myself as she blushed at my look over.
"Have you spoken to Lexi recently?" I wanted to punch myself for asking after I saw the disappointment in her face at my question.
"No." She looked around the restaurant. "Did you want to ask me something about her?"
"No." I wracked my brain for something to say. "Actually, I wanted to talk to you about something else. Something Lexi

can't know about."
"Oh?" She frowned and looked at me with a disconcerted look. "You didn't cheat with someone else as well, did you?"
"No." I frowned. Did she really think that lowly of me? For some reason it really hurt me to hear her ask that question. It was ridiculous that I should feel bad about it but I couldn't stop the jab of pain that ran through me.
"Okay." She wiped her brow. "I was about to say."
"Do you want to know something? I feel like my mom is here with me." I looked down, embarrassed at my honesty. I was scared that she would think I was crazy.
"You do?" She leaned towards me.
"Yeah. Does that sound strange? I feel like my mom is guiding me into doing something to change my life."
"That doesn't sound strange. I talk to my mom every night." She looked away quickly. "I hope you don't think I'm crazy."
"I don't." I smiled at her gently. "I wish I could talk to my mom as well."
"She's my best friend. I've never told anyone that before. Not even Lexi. I guess it's 'cos you know how it feels." She glanced at me quickly. "It's really hard to lose a parent. I don't think people get it until it happens to them."
"Does the pain ever go away?" I clenched my hands, determined not to cry. I'm a man, I shouldn't let every little thing bring me to tears.
"Not really. It lessens. But there isn't a day that goes past that I don't think of her. It gets hard sometimes, because I was so young when she died. I can't always picture her face and it makes me scared, but then I just look at a photo."
"I think about my mom every minute of the day." I looked into my shake. "There isn't a moment that I don't hear her

voice or see her smile. She was the only one who truly loved me from day one." My throat choked up and I looked away.
"She's not the only one who will ever love you though Bryce." She grabbed my hand and squeezed. "I think you of all guys won't have a problem finding love."
"You speak as though it's in the future." I laughed.
"You speak as though she's the only one who's ever loved you." She replied to the question not spoken and I nodded my head.
"You know, Anna, you see yourself as a wallflower who no one sees and I see myself as the guy that everyone sees and no one really knows."
"You're the guy everyone wants to be, Bryce." She tapped her fingers against the table. "And the guy every girl wants to be with."
"Not if they knew what my life was really like." I sighed. "No one would want to be me, or be with me, then."
"You have Lexi."
"I don't know about that." I sighed. "I don't know if I ever really had her."
"It's like you were made for each other. It's the story we all want to believe when we're in high school. The popular quarterback falls for the shy, studious one. Haven't you seen the movies, Bryce? Your reality is everyone's fantasy."
"But that's the problem, Anna, don't you see? This isn't a movie and it's not reality. We're not in high school anymore. I'm far from the blonde jock that everyone wants to be with. I'm just a regular fucked up guy. I'm nobody's Prince Charming. In fact, I'm more akin to the evil wolf."
"You're one handsome evil wolf, Bryce Evans."
"But I'm still a wolf, Anna. I'm still a wolf."

"Yeah, maybe you are." She smiled at me sadly and, once again, I was taken aback by her complete and utter honesty, even when she knew what she was saying may hurt me. I respected that about her.

"So tell me Anna. Why me?" I cocked my head and licked my lips.

"I suppose you think I'm the evil? The jealous kooky best friend." She sighed. "I know it doesn't seem like it, but I regret that night more than anything, it was a horrible thing to do. I've got issues with Lexi, but that wasn't the way to deal with them."

"I don't think you're evil. I'm the last one to pass judgment on anybody." She laughed then, an energized, deep, from the gut laugh and I was happy to see that she was no longer down on herself. "That makes me feel better, Bryce. You are the last person to judge me for what happened." She wiped tears away from her eyes.

"I want to ask you a question, Anna."

"Sure."

"Do you think I would make a good dad?"

"A dad?" Her eyes widened. "Is this a random subject change or what?"

"Yeah." I laughed and leaned towards her."Would you be happy if I was your child's father?"

"Are you asking me to have a kid, Bryce?" She asked me, only half joking.

"No. I just wanted a third party view on how they think I would be as a dad."

"But I don't really know you." She made a face.

"Well, from what you know?"

"I don't know. I'm sorry."

"Hey, don't be sorry." I sighed. It was true. She most probably wanted to tell me no. I mean, it wasn't like she

knew anything good about me."
"I just don't know you that well. Not everyone should have a kid." She looked away from me.
"That's true." I looked at a Disney photo on the wall next to our table. "I think I'd be a good brother, though. I'd do whatever I can to make her happy. I'd be her family. It's what my mom would have wanted. She's old enough to go to kindergarten while I take classes and I can work from home. I can make this work." I chattered excitedly.
"Wait what?" Anna interrupted me. "Brother or father? I'm confused here."
I looked at her in shock. In my excitement I had spoken too much. "I can't talk about it, Anna."
"I'm so confused." She shook her head. "Maybe you can just take me home?"
"It's my sister." I blurted out. I didn't want to be alone. Not now. I needed to talk to someone. "You can't tell anyone. But I have a little sister. I can barely believe it as I say the words. I want to adopt her."
"Wow.
"She's Lexi's sister as well. My dad is the father and her mom is the mom."
"What?!?!" Her jaw dropped and I realized that she didn't know about the affair.
"She never told you?"
"There are many things that Lexi and I never shared," she sighed. "So how old is your sister?"
"Four, I think, maybe five."
"So this happened while we were in high school?"
"Yeah."
"It's funny, isn't it? In high school we think that our lives are going to end if something doesn't go our way. Little do we know that there's a whole world waiting for us to show

us that there's not a lot that's going to go our way."
"That's pretty deep."
"For a girl from Jonesville?" She laughed and I stared at the length of her throat. And then the curve of her lips. She's not the most beautiful girl I've ever seen, but she has a lot more character than I've ever witnessed.
"I'm surprised you didn't tell me I'd make a great dad."
"You mean lie?" She raised an eyebrow.
"Yeah, even if to protect my feelings. I feel like Lexi would have told me I could do anything."
"I bet she would have."
"But it's not true. And it's a lot of responsibility to live up to."
"What is?" She took a sip of her drink and I watched as her tongue darted in and out of her mouth as she sipped. *Look away, Bryce,* I lectured myself, internally. What was I doing? I was not attracted to Anna. I could not let this situation become even more complicated than it was.
"Being the perfect guy. It's a nice label. But it's a hell of a lot to live up to."
"I don't think anyone thinks you're the perfect guy anymore, Bryce." She laughed and I felt like she had slapped me in the face.
"I can be a good guy."
"I'm sure." She smiled. "Every guy can be good."
"You don't think so?"
"I don't know." She sighed. "Life is never what we think it's going to be. And neither are people."
"You know, Anna, you're a lot more different than I thought you were as well."
"Like you ever thought of me before."
"Sure I have." I lied, not wanting to make her feel bad.
"No, no you haven't." She gave me a half smile. "And

that's okay. Maybe I never wanted to be noticed. I didn't want to be the poor kid with the dead mom."
"I'm the poor kid with the dead mom now."
"Oh Bryce, I'm so sorry." Her face collapsed as she realized what she had said.
"It's okay." And in my heart it was. "I like you, Anna."
"I like you too, Bryce."
"Maybe we can go for another shake again soon?"
"I don't think so." She shook her head and sighed and I felt a pang of regret at her words. "I don't want to do this to Lexi. No matter what happens to our friendship."
"We're just hanging out."
"I'd like you to take me home, please." She stood up and I had an overwhelming urge to beg her to stay with me. "Oh and Bryce, I think you'll make a fine big brother or dad. You're a good guy."
"You're just saying that 'cos you want a ride home."
"Maybe." She laughed and put her arm through mine as we walked out of the restaurant and to my car. "And maybe I think that you're just a sheep in wolf's clothing."
"You say the sweetest things." I laughed and we drove in silence back to her home. I drove slowly, not wanting to say goodbye. As we got closer to her home, I felt myself feeling emptier and emptier inside.
"Thanks for driving me home." She looked into my eyes as she took off her seatbelt. "I had a good evening." She was nearly out of the car when I pulled her towards me.
"Wait." I grabbed her arm and she looked up at me curiously. I tilted my head down and kissed her urgently. She kissed me back, passionately and I'm surprised at our sexual chemistry. It hadn't felt like this the night I had been wasted and out of my mind. I felt bereft when she pulled away from me and left my car. I sat there, watching her

walk away and I wanted to get out and run up to her. But I knew there's nothing I could say to make this alright.
I sighed as my phone rang and I was sure it was my dad, calling to discuss the funeral. I was surprised to see Lexi's name on the screen. I felt a slight dread as I answered the phone. I was so confused about everything.
"Hey."
"Hi." Her voice was soft. "Are you okay?"
"Yeah." I sighed. "I'm sorry to drop that bomb on you. I didn't mean to hurt you."
"It's okay. I understand why you said it."
"We should talk."
"Yeah. I think we should talk." She sounded worried and I felt my breath catch. I couldn't end it now. Not after everything she's done for me. Not after she's loved me soo long. I knew in my heart of hearts that she wasn't the one. She had made me believe in myself again, but someone else was winning my heart. But I wasn't going to go back on my word now. I owed her that much. I would stay with her. I would be the man that she needed me to be because that was what I was. I was a man.

Chapter 9
Lexi

I leafed through Bryce's letters after we got off the phone. It seemed like it had been in another universe when they had meant so much to me. It seemed like a dream world and I had woken up. I was now in my real life and everything felt more real and rawer. I thought that finding true love would heal every hurt in my life. But it hadn't. I still felt slightly empty inside. I knew it was because of the conversation I'd heard. I didn't know whom Luke was whispering to, or what it was about, but I knew there was something he wasn't telling me. That one, one-sided phone call had crushed me. I had been flying high until that moment and now I felt low.

I felt even lower now that I had spoken to Bryce. What sort of person would I be if I were to meet up with him and dump him after his mother had died? I couldn't be that person. I was all he had left. He loved me. I didn't know how to tell him that I didn't feel the same way. Not after everything. Maybe I wasn't meant to find love.

The man I loved was lying to me. I never thought Luke would lie to me. Or hide things from me. I didn't want him to throw his life away either. His comments about not going to Boston because of me really distressed me. In another age I would have seen it as the ultimate in love. But now I saw it in a different light. I didn't want to be the one who was responsible for him not following his dream. But I also knew that I didn't want to move to Boston.

"Lexi, can I come in?" My mom opened the door before waiting for me to answer.

"What's up, Mom?"

"I met someone," she giggled, happily.

“Okay and what about it?” I sighed. Here was another relationship that was going to end in tears and heartache for my mother, I thought.
“He wants to marry me.”
“What?” I shrieked in shock. “How long have you known this guy?”
“He gave me a ring.” She pushed her hand towards my face and a huge diamond on her finger blinded my eyes.
“Mom, I didn’t even know you were dating someone. What’s going on here?”
“I’ve known him for a while.” She giggled.
“Who is it, Mom?” I feel my blood run cold as I think of Bryce’s dad. *Please don’t let it be the mayor, please don’t let it be the mayor,* I thought to myself.
“Nate Forester,” she giggled.
“Your boss?” I frowned. “I didn’t even know you were dating him.”
“We weren’t, but he loves me and he says that he wants to take care of me.”
“So what are you going to do mom?” I frowned, worried that I wasn’t going to like what she was going to say.
“I’m going to move in with him of course. After we get married.”
“What about me?”
“You’re a big girl.” She ruffled my hair.
“What am I supposed to do mom, where am I going to live?”
“You can live here.”
“I can’t afford the rent by myself mom.” I felt like I was about to come apart inside.
“You don’t have to pay rent, silly, we own the house.”
“No, we don’t.” I frowned. “Mom, we pay rent.”
“No, we don’t.” She peered at me curiously and shook her

head. "You really don't know, do you?"
"Know what?"
"He gave me the money. He said to use it to buy the house. I thought that was quite rude. I really wanted a new outfit, but he said he spoke to the landlord and asked how much it would cost to buy the house."
"He gave you the money?" I looked at her in shock.
"Yeah, I figured he felt guilty or something. So I bought the house."
"Oh my God, Mom. Why didn't you tell me?"
"I was embarrassed. I…" I didn't hear the rest of her words because I was running out of my house and to my car, with my heart beating fast. Bryce had given my mom the money to buy the house. *He must really love me,* I thought. I knew he was most probably trying to atone for the hurt his father had put my mother through.
I felt disgusted with myself. I couldn't believe that I had betrayed him like this, when he had been working behind my back to make everything right. I knew that I had to put him first. I had to put him before my own personal feelings. I already knew that it was unlikely that I could be fixed, I was most probably destined for a life of not feeling quite whole, but at least I could be there for him. That would be enough for me. That could be a life I grew to love.
My heart hurt thinking about never being with Luke again. But I knew it was the best for him as well. He needed someone better than me. He needed to go to Boston and follow his destiny. I was only holding him back. And I couldn't do that. I knew that I loved him enough to set him free. No matter what he was hiding from me, I knew that Luke was the kindest man in the universe. He would always be in my heart, but I knew that Bryce needed me more and I owed him. We were linked together now, forever. He'd put

too much out there on the line for me. I couldn't leave him in his time of need.

***

I drove with the radio off. I didn't feel too much like singing. As I drove past the psychic's house, I realized she had taken her signs down from the road and the top of her house. I wondered to myself how she had gotten up there. She seemed a bit too old to be going up a ladder.

I was just about to round the corner, when I saw Luke on the next block up, talking to an older man. I pulled over to the side of the road quickly, thankful for once that I lived in a quiet town that didn't have much traffic. I watched as the two men talked animatedly. Luke was shaking his head back and forth and he looked upset. I felt something in my stomach tighten. I'd never seen him look so angry before. The man placed an arm on Luke's shoulder and he shoved it off. I picked up my phone to call Luke to make sure he was okay. I was glad to see that he answered it, instead of just ignoring me. I always knew I could count on Luke.

"Hiya, sweet pea," he purred into the phone. He was a better actor than I thought. I could see that he was still glaring at the man he was with.

"Hey, I was just thinking about you," I said, breathlessly.

"I'm glad you called me then." He paused. "I wanted to talk to you about Boston again."

"Luke, I don't want to discuss this right now." I sighed.

"I'm not going to let you not go."

"Oh Lexi." I could hear the frustration in his voice. "I never want to be where you aren't."

"We can't always have what we want." I bit my lip. "Can I come over now so we can talk?"

“I’m just at the store.” He lied easily and I gasped. “But maybe you can come over in about an hour?”
“What are you getting at the store?”
“You know, the usual: chocolates, wine, cookies. Everything you love.”
“Huh—it sounds awfully quiet in Hy-Vee today.”
“Well, you know. Everyone must have gone shopping on Saturday,” he said, smoothly. “But I have to go now. See you later.”
“Yeah, I’ll see you later.”
“I love you, Lexi.”
“I love you too, Luke,” I said, sadly. I couldn’t believe that he had lied to me again. It was as if the universe was telling me that no guy was good and that I should honor my commitment to Bryce, even though we didn’t have any formal commitment really.
I sighed and watched Luke continue talking to the men and then, finally, the man took a folder out of a brown leather bag and handed it to Luke. Luke seemed happy then and shook his hand. I watched him look around quickly before quickly walking back to his car. I sat frozen in my car as he left and watched as the older man walked into a building. As Luke drove off, I put my car into drive again and drove up slowly to see which building the old man had come out from.
I was surprised to see a lawyer’s sign on the front. Why would Luke need to see a lawyer? It had to be something important for him to have looked so anxious and angry. And why would he lie about it? What was it that Luke didn’t want anyone knowing about? And why had he and Bryce been at the hospital together? Had it been a coincidence that they had both been there at the same time? My mind was rambling with questions and I was

determined to get some answers.
I looked at my watch and pressed my foot down on the acceleration. I was late. I drove quickly to make up time and arrived at Harpers Creek about fifteen minutes late. Bryce was already out of his car when I got there and I jumped out and ran to the riverbank to meet up with him.
"You made it." He turned to me with a small smile and we hugged briefly.
"Yeah, sorry. I got held up."
"No worries. I was just watching the fish."
"Oh?" I looked into the water but didn't see anything asides from some dead branches and leaves floating.
"Do you ever wonder what it's like to be a fish? What they must be thinking about. What they think when they see a worm? Do you think they wonder to themselves, *I hope this worm doesn't have a hook attached?*"
I shook my head at Bryce's words. I can honestly say those thoughts had never crossed my mind.
"It's kind of funny, you know. That a fish wouldn't have figured it out already. I know there's all kind of bait, but really a worm is like a sign to the fish. The worm is begging the fish to see it and think, *I don't normally see worms underwater. This must be a trap.* But no, the fish is as greedy as any human being. He doesn't use his brain and think trap, he just sees instant food and goes for it."
I nodded my head. He had a point, I suppose. "Is this an analogy then? Fish are as greedy as humans?"
"No. More like a warning for life. Maybe we should think critically before we make any actions. You know?"
"Yeah. I do." I sighed and looked down at the ground.
"But sorry to bore you. How are you?" He rubbed my shoulder and I tried not to flinch at his touch. As I looked into his handsome face, I was once again amazed at just

how perfect looking he was. His blue eyes are so wide and open. So pure and innocent and the gold tints in his blond hair, shone like they had been polished. As I stared at him, I can see why the younger me had been infatuated with him. He was everything a girl like me could dream of.

"I'm good. A little tired. How are you feeling?"

"Tired. Frantic. Angry. All cried out. Despondent." He cracked a half-smile. "But I'm also hopeful. Really hopeful. I think that I can take charge of my life. You know. With all the love and support you've given me. That you've always given me."

I gulp as he talks. So this was it then. He needed me. I was stuck to him at this point. It was my duty and obligation to provide him strength now.

"I'm glad you have hope." I looked away quickly. I felt the tell tale signs of burning in my eyes. I knew that I was about to cry.

"I'm sorry about Anna." His voice broke as he said her name. I realized that he must have been really despondent. "I shouldn't have let it happen."

"You don't have to apologize." I was in no position to pass judgment now that I'd slept with Luke. My darling precious Luke.

"It was wrong. I'll spend the rest of my life making it up to you, Lexi."

I couldn't stop the tears as they sprung from my eyes. The rest of his life. The rest of my life. With Bryce. I couldn't imagine it. What was a life if I had to be with someone I didn't love?

"Lexi, are you okay?" He brought me in close to him and I sobbed into his shoulders. I couldn't let him know that these tears were for Luke and me. It wasn't his fault. He wasn't to know that I'd been living in a fantasy world and

that the love of my life had been next door all along. “Lexi, look at me. Are you okay?” He pulled my face up to look at his and we stood there staring at each other, wordlessly. He leaned down to kiss me and we stood there with our arms around each other, but unable to bring our two lips together.
“Lexi, you should know that Anna and I went out for shakes last night.” He let out a deep sigh. “I didn’t mean to hurt you. I just thought that she needed a friend.”
“It’s okay.” I look at him in wonder. “You know Anna’s not a bad person. I haven’t been the best friend she has needed in a long time.”
“She’s really funny,” he said, wistfully. “I never knew that she was so funny and honest.”
“She is isn’t she? And she’s a good listener.”
“I know.” He sat down on the grass and I joined him. “Has she ever had a real boyfriend?”
“No, not really.” I leaned back and stared at the sky. “Neither of us has really. We were both just too busy dreaming and planning.”
“Creating castles out of clouds?”
“Yeah.” I picked a piece of grass and played with it in my fingers. “We were great at building castles. Maybe too good.”
“Why do you say that?”
“Our whole lives we’ve created fantasies of men we thought we wanted to be with. We’ve built everything up in our imagination, nothing can ever compare to that. You know? Daydreams are all good and well but not at the sake your life. Not when the love you build up in your head isn’t really real. I loved you and Anna loved Eddie and we spent all of high school in some alternate reality where our biggest hopes and dreams were based on whether one of you talked to us.” I sighed heavily.

"Eddie was gay, you know," he blurted out and I rolled over in surprise.
"What?"
"He was gay," he sighed. "I didn't really know until right before he died. He made a move at me. Said some things. I didn't know how to react." He tensed. "I was uncomfortable and confused. And I felt like I didn't even know him anymore. I'm so mad that I made it about me. I can only imagine how much worse he had felt, coming clean to me."
"But he tried to rape me?" I frowned. "That doesn't make sense."
"I think he was trying to make a man out of himself. I think he was trying to prove to himself that he liked women. I think he was drunk and confused. And he was trying to prove his love to me in some way. I was soo angry at you," Bryce sighed. "I'm not really sure exactly. But I fucked up. I fucked up by trying to get revenge on you and I fucked up when he told me he was gay. I didn't know what to think. I'm not homophobic but, you know, I just acted really badly."
"It's still not your fault he killed himself, Bryce." I reached over and held his hands. "It seems like he had a lot of demons."
"I know. But I certainly didn't help. And I will have to face that knowledge for the rest of my life. Anyways, I just thought it was important to say. Anna thinks that he didn't like her because she's not pretty enough, but it had nothing to do with her looks. He, he just wasn't into women. I, I wanted her to know that. But I don't really know if I should say anything. I don't know if she is still in love with him?"
Something in me twitched as he spoke. It was in the way he had said Anna's name and the way his eyes had glazed over

that made me think that he had some sort of feeling for her. More than just concern that she know that Eddie hadn't dissed her because he hadn't thought she was cute enough.
"She's really pretty, you know. I mean, I guess I can see how she can feel like second best, being friends with you; she's one of those girls you have to really get to know to fully appreciate her. But she's beautiful. I wish she knew it." He laughed, nervously. "I'm sorry for talking about her still. I just wish she knew how beautiful she really is."
"Bryce, I'm going to ask you something." I looked at him, seriously. "I want you to answer honestly, okay?"
"Okay." He swallowed hard and I could tell he was nervous.
"Do you like Anna?"
"What?" He looked at me with a shocked expression and I held a hand up.
"I just want the truth, please. It's okay." I held my breath as I waited for his answer. This could be the answer to all my prayers I thought. This could be the key to us both letting go.
"I don't know how it happened, Lexi." He looked away. "I just feel like we have a special connection. Maybe it's because both of our mom's are dead."
I tried to hide the smile that was spreading across my face. "So you like Anna, right?"
"I'll still marry you, Lexi. I want to be the guy you believed in for all those years."
"I don't love you, Bryce," I spat out before I could stop myself. "I'm sorry and I don't want to hurt you, but I don't love you, not like that. I thought I did. For soo many years, I thought you were the perfect guy and my savior, but it was a dream. There are no perfect guys and there are no saviors. And that's okay. I'm okay with that."

“You don’t love me?” He looked at me with a hurt expression and I was still worried that I had made a huge mistake and misread the situation, but then he started laughing. He was laughing so hard that he started coughing and I looked at him in concern, worried I had pushed him to the breaking point.

“I’m sorry, Bryce.” I peered down at him and he grabbed me and pulled me towards him.

“Oh Lexi Lord, do you know how much I love you right now?” He kissed my cheeks and hugged me hard. “Thank you.” And then he started crying. I could feel his tears running from my hair down my face and dropping on my arms. They were warm and cooling, all at the same time and I just held him as he cried. We lay there for about ten minutes and then Bryce pulled away from me.

“As you can see, I’m a bit of a mess still.”

“Aren’t we all?”

“So you don’t love me, huh?” He grinned at me and I shook my head.

“No. I’m sorry.”

“Don’t be.” He rolled his eyes. “It actually makes me feel better.”

“Because you love Anna?”

He shook his head. “No, no I don’t know if I love Anna.” He laughed. “It makes me feel more comfortable to be myself and make mistakes.”

“Huh?”

“I felt like you saw me as your Prince Charming. And I’m not. I’m barely an average guy who’s trying to work out his demons. I was worried that you would always be disappointed in the real me.”

“Oh Bryce,” I sigh. “I never wanted you to feel that kind of pressure from me.”

"It's okay." He shook his head and laughed. "And I can't believe I'm going to say this, but I think you should give Luke a chance."
"What?"
"He loves you, Lexi. I don't know if you see it, but he really loves you." I felt my face go red as he spoke and I closed my eyes.
"I have to tell you something." My voice was uncertain. "Please don't hate me."
"What is it, Lexi?" He looked at me, worried.
"I kinda love Luke and we kinda, you know."
His eyes popped open and his mouth dropped. "You didn't?"
I nodded, embarrassed and worried. I didn't want him to be angry with me. I knew that I should have waited to have a conversation with Bryce before I let myself go into Luke's arms.
"Wow." He laughed and shook his head. "No wonder Luke was acting so cagey."
"Bryce, I want to ask you something. And I need you to tell me the truth."
"Of course, Lexi."
"Why were you and Luke at the hospital together the other day?"
"You know about that?" His eyes looked worried and he sat up. "You haven't told anyone about that have you?"
"No." I sigh, anxiously. "I only know because I overheard a conversation Luke had with someone."
"He didn't tell you?"
"No. Why do you think I'm asking you?"
"I told him not to say anything." He sighed. "I can't afford for it to get out."
"For what to get out, Bryce?"

"I suppose you have a right to know."
"To know what?" I was losing patience.
"Do you remember that little girl we met in the hospital the other day. Shelby?"
I shook my head in confusion. "No, what little girl?"
The girl in the room when you fainted. You know, when you saw Luke. I wracked my brain and tried to remember a little girl and a vague memory popped up. "I think so. Why?"
"Well, I'm not sure how to say this."
"Is she your kid Bryce?"
"No." He laughed. "No."
"Oh my God, she's Luke's kid isn't she? He lied to me? He told me he never had sex. I wondered how he was so good." Oops. I blushed at my words. "That's why he hasn't told me? He's scared of what I'll do if I find out he has a kid?"
"That's quite a story, Lexi but no, that's not it either." Bryce laughed and I sighed with relief. "Shelby's our sister, Lexi."
"What?" I stared at him, flabbergasted. "What did you just say?"
"The kid your mom gave up. That's Shelby. She had cancer. My mom was going to adopt her and now I'm trying to."
"Wait, what?" I tried to grasp everything he was saying. "You found our sister?"
"I didn't find her." He paused. "But she is our sister."
"How do you know?" I frowned.
"Luke told me."
"What?" I jumped up. "What do you mean? When? How did he even know?"
"He did some work at the orphanage. He saw the records," Bryce sighed. "Don't be mad with him, Lexi."

"But I never told him my mom had a kid. Never. I was too ashamed. And he knew I was lying the whole time. He just pretended he didn't know." The tears popped up again. "How could he do this to me?" My heart was pounding and I felt like I wanted the ground to open up and swallow me.
"Lexi, I'm positive he didn't do this to hurt you."
"What is he? Your best friend now?" I turned away from him and started walking back to my car. "Are you the reason why he went to go and see a lawyer as well? Is he helping you to get our sister behind my back?" I shouted as I started to run.
"Wait, what?" Bryce ran after me. "What are you talking about? What lawyer?"
"I saw Luke talking to a lawyer on the street, that's why I was late today."
"Do you remember what street you were on, or the name of the law firm?" He frowned.
"No, not really."
"This is really important, Lexi, please." He ran his hands through his hair and his golden ends looked all spiky. "I have been speaking to a lawyer about adopting Shelby, but I've been keeping it hush hush because I know if my father finds out, he'll get Shelby shipped away somewhere. I haven't asked Luke to help me with anything, Lexi." He sounded panicked. "I hope my dad didn't get to him."
"Luke wouldn't do that." I frowned though. I was no longer sure that I really knew Luke all that well anymore.
"The lawyer told me that my application is pretty strong but the only problem is I don't have my own house and I am not very liquid."
"Oh Bryce." I grabbed him. "This is all my fault isn't it?"
"No, of course not."
"Yes it is. If you hadn't given my mom the money to buy

the house then you would have had a stronger application."
"What?" He frowned at me.
"I can never thank you enough for doing that for me and my mom, Bryce. I'll pay you every month until I repay the loan. I promise."
"Lexi, I don't know what you're talking about. I never gave your mom any money. Certainly not enough to buy a house."
"What? It wasn't you?" My mind started ticking over and over and I frowned. "Then who?"
"I don't know, Lexi, but I think we need to pay a visit to my attorney."
"Do you think we could visit Shelby as well?" I asked a bit nervously. "I'd like to see her."
"Of course. She's wonderful, Lexi. I just love her so much already."
"Does she know about us?" I question curiously.
"No," he sighed. "But maybe we should tell her today."
"Are you sure? What if everything doesn't work out well?"
"I think she needs to know the truth. No matter what happens." Bryce looked determined. "I want her to know the truth."
"Okay." I nodded my head and my breath caught as a butterfly circled around me and then landed on my hand. It had wings of red, black and gold and I was mesmerized by its beauty and bravery. "Hello." I whispered and then it flew away. I noticed that the sun had also come out. And I felt a fresh burst of energy and verve. This is a new beginning for me I thought. This is the time for me to start my life afresh: to live in the here and now.

Chapter 10
Bryce

I didn't want Lexi to see how panicked I was, but my heart was in my throat as I drove to my lawyer's office. Luke was probably the most trustworthy man I had ever met, but I knew how devious and calculated my father could be. If he had any clue that I was trying to adopt his illegitimate daughter he would do everything in his power to shut it down. Even someone like Luke might find it hard to say no.
I parked quickly and waited impatiently for Lexi to get out of her car. She looked at me, with worried eyes, as she looked at the office. "This is where he came earlier."
"I see." I tried to quell my fears. "Let's go in."
"Okay." She looked worried and I knew that she was also wondering what Luke could have done.
"I'm here to see Mr. Raynor, please." I spoke sharply to the secretary.
"He's on a call, Sir."
"Tell him that it's Bryce Evans and it's really important."
"Can you take a seat, Sir?"
"No. I need you to tell him now."
"Okay." She rolled her eyes and stood up before knocking on a door and walking into David Raynor's office.
"Come on." I grabbed Lexi and walked to the office. I pushed the door aside and walked in with Lexi standing next to me, reluctantly.
"Mr. Evans, I told you that…" the secretary looked at me angrily.
"Have a seat, Bryce." David waved me towards the chairs. "It's okay, Margaret. I'll speak to Bryce."
"Yes, Sir." She glared at me before she exited the office. I saw Lexi looking at me with trepidation on her face. I knew

exactly what she was scared about. I squeezed her hand and we waited for the lawyer to finish his phone call. She smiled at me quickly and squeezed my hand back and I sent up a quick prayer that at least something in my life was going right. Lexi and I were going to remain friends, even though our romance had fizzled out as soon as it had begun. Maybe my mom was in heaven looking out for me, I thought. She'd be happy to see that we had talked about our feelings honestly.

"Okay, Bryce, how can I help you?"

"I want to know why Luke Bryan was here today. And I want to know what's going on with Shelby." I leaned forward and stared into his eyes. "And I want to know the truth."

To my surprise, David Raynor put his head in his hands and sighed. A long deep heavy sigh. And then he looked back up at me. "Who's this then?" He nodded towards Lexi and she stood up and offered him her hand.

"I'm Lexi Lord. I'm Shelby's sister."

"I see." The lawyer sat down and sighed. "Oh what a tangled web we weave when at first we start to deceive."

"Sorry, what?"

"Nothing." He sighed again. "I can't tell you why Luke was here. Unfortunately that is attorney client privilege."

"Is he working for my dad?" I shouted. "Is he trying to stop me from adopting Shelby?"

"What?" He laughed, and I could see amusement in his eyes. "No, no, Luke is far from working for your dad."

"What is he doing then?" Lexi leaned forward and spoke in hushed tones. "I don't want to invade his privacy, but I have to know. Is he in trouble?"

"No, no he's not." David played with the files on his desk and looked up with a troubled expression on his face. "I've asked him to tell you. But he doesn't want to. It's his own choice. I personally think it's best for everything to be out in the open. It's time. Let the chips fall where they may."

"What are you talking about, David?" I sighed, not understanding what he was saying.

"Even the mighty have to fall at some time. But it's not my decision to make. Luke will do what he wants." He looked me in the eye then. "But you should know that he is not trying to stop you from adopting Shelby. He is actually trying to help you. He set up a trust in Shelby's name. And he named you as the conservator. He is willingly to openly support you and your quest."

"What?" A cold sliver of shock ran through me. "What? Why?"

"He wants to see Shelby looked after and he thinks you will make a good older brother and father figure to her."

"But I don't understand." I frowned. "He can't just give you money like that."

"Is that why he came to see you?" Lexi whispered.

"No. That wasn't the main reason he came to see me. But he inquired about your adoption process. He knows I have a close relationship with the orphanage and the powers that be. He wanted to know what the likelihood was of you being able to adopt Shelby."

"And what did you say?"

"I told him what I told you. You were a good candidate but you don't have your own abode or a stable source of income."

"And then he just gave you a huge chunk of money?" I frowned in disbelief.

"He asked me if I could create a trust for Shelby with some monies he would donate. He asked to name you as conservator and he said he would publicly support the

adoption."
"But how would that help?" Lexi looked as taken aback as I felt.
"They love him at the orphanage. He's one of their success stories. He got adopted at age six but he never forgot them. He has been volunteering there for years. In fact, when he made his first million, his first major donation was to them."
"His first million?" Lexi frowned. "He has millions?"
I was just as surprised. "Luke was adopted?" I turned to Lexi and I saw she that she was frozen still with huge eyes.
"I never knew he was adopted." She blinked and looked at me, blankly. "He never told me he was adopted."
"I've said too much." David Raynor looked worried. "I can't talk much longer. Both of you should know that Luke only has your best interests at heart."
"What does he want?" I stare at the files on David's table. "I don't understand it. Why would he do this for me? It doesn't make any sense."
"Luke has his reasons." David stood up. "And now, I really need to get to some work."
"Did Luke buy my mom's house?" Lexi had tears in her eyes as she questioned the lawyer. "He bought my mom's house didn't he?"
The lawyer nodded. "Yes."
"Why?"
"You need to ask him dear." David looked at both of us apologetically. "Maybe you both need to speak to Luke. He's a good man. He looks after his family. He's a good man." And, just like that, Lexi and I are out of his office. We stood there staring at each other with shocked expressions on our faces.
"I guess I really don't know Luke do I?" Lexi's lips

trembled as she played with her hair. “Why didn’t he tell me?”
“Because he loves you.” I was hesitant as I talked, trying to find the right words to explain it to her and myself. “I think he loves you so much that he just wants you to be happy. And, no matter what, he wants you to be okay. He wants to make sure, as best as he can, that you are okay. What a man. He did this for you when he thought you were in love with me.”
“He shouldn’t have done it!” she cried out.
“He did it because you have his heart. You really and truly have his heart.” And then I frowned. “I don’t understand why he would do this for me though. He doesn’t owe me anything.”
“Maybe he did it for Shelby.” We left the office and stood by the big oak tree, instead of getting directly into our cars. “He obviously loves her. And maybe, because you’re her brother, he saw it as the best way to make sure she is happy.”
“But he doesn’t know me.” I frowned. “I was an ass in high school. We weren’t friends and I can’t think he even likes me now, after what happened between you and me. So why would he trust me? It doesn’t make sense.”
“Maybe because he knows what it’s like to be adopted? What it’s like to be given a forever family with people who love him?”
“He has a good family?” I question, wondering what his childhood had been like; wondering about the sort of parents it took to raise a man as good as him.
She nodded and smiled. “They’re wonderful. They support him in everything he does and he does everything he can for them. I guess I understand now, why they seem to appreciate and love him more than life itself. They most

probably feel blessed to have a son like him."
"He's a great guy." And then I laughed and she looked at me confused.
"What's so funny?"
"How did you pick the two of us? He's Mr. Perfect and I'm the exact opposite. I've got a shitty family, I've spent most of my life worrying about myself and—"
"—Stop." She put her finger to my lips. "I never want to hear you doubting yourself again, Bryce. The past is the past. We've all made mistakes. But as long as we recognize them and we move on and try to do better in our lives, it's okay. No one's perfect, Bryce. Not even Luke. Never put yourself down. You're a good guy."
"Do you really think so?" I looked to the sky. "Sometimes I wonder if I will ever truly be a man my mom can truly be proud of. Sometimes I don't know if I am coming or going."
"We all feel that way, Bryce." She smiled softly. "I think that's a part of life."
"You mean this feeling will never go away?"
"I don't know. But it can't be bad can it? To question and to never stop the journey to being a better person."
"I guess not. I guess we're growing up now huh, Lexi?"
"It's weird." She laughed. "But I think we are. I don't see you as the hot quarterback anymore and myself as the invisible flower."
"You were never invisible." I stroked her cheek. "But I do take offense at no longer being considered the hot quarterback."
"Oh you're still hot. Just not in a 'I hope he asks me to Prom' way." She laughed and I took her hand and pulled her closer to me.
"I hope you never change, Lexi. I want you to sing Disney

songs at the top of you voice, I want you to write letters of hope and love to any and everyone you want to, I want you to laugh and dance and scream and shout. I want you to keep believing in your dreams."

"I don't know, Bryce. Dreams aren't always what they seem. Maybe I need to just come down to earth once and for all."

"Lexi, if you didn't dream we would never be here." My voice was husky. "And I wouldn't be here. I wouldn't be functioning right now, Lexi." I closed my eyes and I pictured my mom's face. "I wouldn't have made it Lexi."

"Yes you would have."

"No." I shook my head. "No, not like this."

"Are you going to ask Anna to date you?" She grinned at me and I laughed at her eagerness.

"Now, that's a slightly awkward question." I laughed and shrugged. "I don't know." I felt a spark of electricity run through me as I thought about Anna. "I like her a lot but I don't know if this is the time to try and start a relationship. I need to focus on myself now."

"Wow, look at us. Two strong, single people."

"What?" I frowned as she attempted a smile. "What about Luke?"

"I feel like I don't even really know him." Her voice trailed off. "He's so much more than I ever knew and I ache inside, Bryce. Why didn't he tell me, oh, so many things?"

"But you didn't tell him everything either, Lexi, that's not fair."

"Life has a way of not being fair."

"Don't be hardheaded, Lexi. Don't become bitter. Your best quality is your big heart."

"Eh, I don't know about that."

"Trust me."

“Okay.” She rolled her eyes and I laughed.
“Dear Bryce, I know you don’t know me but I wanted you to know that I think you’re a wonderful human being. I know you may be hurting right now and I know you may think that you have no one, but I want you to know that I’m someone who thinks a lot of you. I’m someone who cares and I just want you to know. That I pray for your safety every night. Stay safe, my dearest Bryce. Miss.” My voice trembled as I tried to remember her letter accurately and she looked at me with wide eyes.
“You memorized my letter?”
“Pretty much all of them.” I ran my hand through my hair, embarrassed. “It was quite easy really. I read them soo many times.”
“You did?”
“They meant the world to me Lexi.” I tried to explain how they had made me feel. “You reached me at the darkest point in my life. I didn’t know if I wanted to live, but your letters, your kind, beautiful letters, they saved me. I think that’s why I thought I loved you.”
“Words are powerful.” She nodded. “I understand.” She still had a sad look on her face and I sighed.
“Let’s go see Shelby. She’ll cheer you up. I promise.”
“I’m ready.” She looked at me nervously. “I hope she likes me.”
“She’ll love you. Of that I’m sure.”

Chapter 11
Lexi

I was grinning like an idiot when I got home. Shelby was a beautiful and loving child who had embraced Bryce and I immediately. The doctor had stayed in the room as we told her the news, just to make sure she wasn't overwhelmed, and I saw a few tears in his eyes as she had yelped with pleasure and given us a huge hug upon hearing we were her family.
"You're my brother and sister?" She had looked back and forth at us with amazement in her eyes.
"Yes Shelby." Bryce had held her soo tenderly. I'd never seen him look that happy before. Never seen such a light in his eyes. "I'd like to adopt you as well, if you'd like that."
She had nodded happily, clinging to his arm. I could tell that that had delighted Bryce. Here was someone who really, truly needed him. And loved him for who he was. He had a chance to start over. To be the man he always wanted to be. To be a man he could be proud of.
I laughed as I got out of the car. Maybe it was just as well that Bryce and I hadn't worked out. I didn't want to be a candidate for the Jerry Springer show, raising my sister with her brother as his lover. That was just a bit too much, even for my lax sensibilities.
"Hey, penny for them?" I heard Luke's voice before I saw him and I fell back into the grass as Bongo came jumping on me. "Bongo, sit. Bongo," Luke commanded the dog, who ignored him as he licked my face. "Sorry."
"It's okay." I laughed as he pulled me up from the grass. "Naughty Bongo."
"I think I need Anna to come help me train him," he laughed and then groaned as he realized what he had said.

"Sorry. I can find someone else."
"No." I shook my head. "It's okay. I need to make amends with Anna anyway."
"You've forgiven her?" He looked at me in surprise.
"I'm not sure that forgiven is the right word." I shook my head. "What she did is a hard thing to get over, but I know I haven't been the perfect friend and I miss her. Sometimes a hurt is about what's beneath the initial shock and pain. I think Anna was hurting a whole lot more than I was."
"I think you're my perfect friend." I felt Luke's lips against mine and they felt so right, the perfect fit. I melted against him and I felt like I had come home when I felt his tongue slip into my mouth. I grasped his hair and pulled his face down so that I was kissing him harder. I didn't want to ever leave this moment. It felt so perfect. His arms slid around my waist and he placed his hands into my back pockets. I giggled as he pinched my ass.
"Luke." I squealed as I pulled away from him and he laughed.
"Yes, Lexi?" His eyes crinkled and I studied his jawline. It's so strong and sturdy, just like him. I knew I would never get tired of staring into his eyes and seeing the love reflected there. There would never be too many soft but intimate touches between us, melding us together. Sometimes when we hugged I didn't know where my body ended and his began. It felt like we were one. One big cosmos in the universe, joined together for life.
"You're going to Boston you know." I spoke softly but firmly, changing the subject.
"No Lexi." He shook his head. "I'm not."
"You have to go to MIT. That's your dream. You've worked so hard for it."
"That's not my dream, Lexi. You are." He pulled me

towards him and kissed my nose. "You've always been my dream." I felt his hand creep up my shirt and, as much as I wanted to make love to him and forget all the worries and concerns that were crowding my brain, I couldn't.
"Luke, I want to know why you went to see a lawyer today." I shot out, unable to keep it inside anymore. "I want to know why you never told me you were adopted. I want to know why you bought this house. I want to know how you can lie to me and love me at the same time." I pushed him away from me and felt bereft as his hand left my breast.
"Lexi." He frowned and shook his head. "I don't even know what to say. How, how did you find out?"
"Bryce and I went to the attorney, David what's-his-face. I saw you earlier. I wanted to know. He wanted to know." My words jumbled together, confusing and choppy.
"You were with Bryce?" He frowned. "You didn't tell me."
"Yes, I ... we ... we needed to talk. I wanted to make sure he was going to be okay. I owed it to him." I took a deep breath, trying to remain calm."And I know about Shelby."
Luke's face showed me that he knew what a big deal it was to keep Shelby a secret from me. "I didn't want to keep her a secret from you, Lexi. But you never told me about your mom and the Mayor. I didn't want to take that from you."
"I was embarrassed." I felt my face flush. "I didn't want you to judge me or my mom. I just wanted to keep it a secret. I don't even know why now."
"You didn't want it to define who you were," he said, softly. "You didn't want her affair to make a difference to your persona and your life."
"Yeah." I looked up at him with unshed tears. "I didn't want to add on another thing to the 'that poor girl' list. I just wanted for us to be us, without that. We've always just

been us. I wanted to keep it normal between us. Equal, you know."
"I understand, Lexi." He sighed. "Sometimes there are things that you just want to keep away from your real main life. Does that make sense?"
"Yeah. I didn't want to think about it or even acknowledge it. But you know it never left my mind. I just dealt with it internally. Or at least I tried to."
"You tried to displace it from your mind because you knew there was nothing positive to it. You knew that your parents loved you with every fiber of your being and that was all you needed. Sometimes hidden secrets and heartaches just need to stay hidden."
"Yeah." I looked at him suddenly. "Wait, what did you say?" I frowned. "Are you talking about me or you, Luke?"
He sighed and sat on the grass and I joined him, glad I hadn't worn a pair of white trousers. "So, I only found out a few years ago." He played with Bongo's ears as he spoke. "I was volunteering at the orphanage. I had created some new software to streamline all the files to make it easier for everyone. That's where I first saw Shelby's file."
"Oh, so that's how you knew." I nodded my head in understanding.
"And then I saw my file." He looked at me with wide eyes. "And I felt a yearning I never knew I felt. You know? My parents, they're the best. But I guess I had always, somewhere deep inside, wondered what had happened to my birth parents. Why they had given me up."
"Oh Luke." I felt my heart go out for him.
"And so I looked in my file. My mom died, giving birth to me. She had been young, barely out of high school. She was beautiful." He smiled. "I saw her photo in an old Jonesville High yearbook."

"You'll have to show me." I brought his hand up to my lips and kissed it. "I'd like to see what your birth mom looked like."

"But then I turned the page and I saw who my mom had listed as my dad. I felt like the world was crashing around me. I wanted to scream and shout. I was so angry!" he shouted.

"You know who he is?" I looked at him in surprise.

He nodded and closed his eyes. "When I realized who my birth father was, I thought I was going to breakdown."

"Who is it?" I stared at Luke with bated breath.

"Lexi, Bryce is my brother. My half brother."

"What?" I frowned. "Wait, your dad is the mayor?"

He nodded and I felt like I was frozen in a dream. How many people had this guy fucked up? "And it all made sense to me. He has many illegitimate kids that he has made women give up, Lexi. I saw the files. You wouldn't believe how many women listed him as the father of their child."

"OMG." I stared at him in shock and as I looked at him I could somewhat see a slight resemblance. I'm not sure if I'm imagining it but if I forgot the cosmetic differences, like hair and eye color, Luke and Bryce had quite the physical resemblance.

"So then I realized that Shelby was also my half-sister and I started to spend more time with her. And that's how Mrs. Evans and I became close."

"She knew as well?"

"I think she suspected," he sighed. "She knew her husband was a dog. She was going to divorce him and adopt Shelby. But she always made small comments to me about having such a wonderful family and things happening for a reason."

"Wow," I gasped.

"And I realized that the best thing that happened to me was being adopted by my parents. I had always had this hole, wondering why my birth parents didn't love me enough to keep me. But the best thing that happened to me was not having the mayor as a father."

"Yeah. Some people shouldn't be parents." I sat back and thought about the words the psychic had told me about my dad. "You know, I think I'm lucky that my dad wasn't in my life as well. He was a meth addict. I don't know if I would have wanted to deal with that." My voice trailed off.

"It makes you wonder doesn't it?"

"What?" I looked at him, curiously.

"It makes you wonder if all the things we complain or worry about are actually blessings in disguise. Maybe we should just be happy with the lot we have and appreciate it."

"You could be right," I laughed. "I had you next door to me all these years, yet my heart always yearned for someone else. Someone who is great but not the one for me."

"Oh?" He grinned at me. "Who is the one for you?"

"I think I'll keep that a secret," I laughed.

"You little terror." He started to tickle me and I could barely breathe.

"Okay, okay, it's you, Luke. It's you. It's always been you." I giggled. "I love you, Luke Bryan. I will always love you." He cuts off my words with his lips and, as we rolled around on the grass, I wondered at the fact that it had taken me so long to realize that he was the man of my dreams.

"So are you going to tell me why you bought this house?"

"I knew that you felt like you had to stay here to support your mom. I knew that as long as you thought your mom needed you to help with the rent you would stay. I wanted you to be able to live your live Lexi. I wanted you to go and leave out your dreams. I wanted you to feel like you could do whatever you wanted to without feeling like you had to stay because of money."

"I don't know what to say Luke. I don't think anyone has ever loved me or cared about me as much as you do." I felt fresh tears glisten in my eyes.

"I want the world for you Lexi." He kissed me again and stared into the very depths of my soul. I felt my heart singing out in joy that I had been so lucky to have found the best man in the world.

"So are you going to tell Bryce?" I questioned him as we stopped kissing.

"I guess I have to tell Bryce and Shelby." He smiled and then I groaned as it hit me.

"OMG, you know what this means, don't you?"

"No, what?"

"We're kinda brother and sister."

"Oh, Lexi." He grinned. "We are nothing like brother and sister." And then his hand crept up to my breast again.

"And in a few minutes I'm going to show you why."

"Luke! I jumped up, squealing. Not outside." I ran away from him, laughing and I heard Luke and Bongo chasing after me.

"I'm coming for you, Lexi." Luke grunted as he chased me.

"I'm going to have my wicked way with you, Lexi."

"I'm waiting." I stopped and winked as he caught up with me.

"Good." Luke laughed as he grabbed a hold of me. "I've been waiting my whole life to hear those words."

"Yeah?" I smiled and he pushed me up against the wall.

"Well, since I was thirteen at least."

"Just thirteen?"

"Well, when you know you know." He stared into my eyes

as he spoke and I felt his breath against my lips as he talked. He turned me on and it took everything in me to keep my hands off of him.

"I'm glad you waited for me to get my act together." I whispered and I felt his lips against mine as I talked.

"I wasn't going anywhere." His hands clasped mine and he blew on my mouth softly.

"I don't think I would have let you go anywhere," I laughed lightly. "But don't you ever die or make me think you've died, do you hear me?"

"I—"

"—I can not have another near breakdown like that." I stared into his eyes, willing him to see my open heart and soul. "I couldn't bare it."

"I won't." Our noses touched and I held my breath. Every nerve ending in me was tingling in anticipation.

"Good." I smiled and pushed my tongue out to lick his lips.

"I wrote a song for you." He looked at me, nervously and sheepishly, and he pulled away from me slightly. I moaned at the loss of his lips. "I remember once you told me how much you wanted someone to write a song for you."

"You wrote a song for me?" I looked at him, teasingly.

"Yes." His face flushed red and I stroked his chin.

"Sing it for me. Please." I ran my hands over his jaw and he groaned.

"If you keep touching me like that, Lexi, I won't be able to do anything."

"Sorry." I grinned. "Sing me my song please."

He cleared his throat and began:

Best friends
That's what we are
Best friends

That's what we'll always be.

There is no me without you.
There is no me without you.

I'll wait a hundred years for your heart
You have to know mine won't start
Without you.

Cos, there is no me without you.
There is no me without you.

I've walked a thousand years for your smile
I've loved you since you were a child.
Always and forever.

There is no me without you.
There is no me without you.

Did you know that sometimes I can close my eyes
And feel your soul in mine
I'll never let you go.

There is no me without you.
There is no me without you.

Lexi, sometimes in life
There are things worth dying for,
People worth fighting for,
A love worth trying for,
And I will never walk out that door, without you.

Cos, there is no me without you.

There will never be a me without you.
I can't live without you.
I can't see without you.
I can't hear without you.
I just can't be without you.
Don't let me live my life without you.

"Oh Luke," I cried out, "That was beautiful."
"I love you, Lexi. That will never stop. I will do anything for you. Always remember that."
"Oh Luke. I'll never forget."
"I'm your albatross, Lexi."
"You never explained what they meant," I laughed anxiously, worried he had finally lost it.
"Albatrosses mate for life. Once they have that one special mate, that's it. They're done. You're my albatross, Lexi. And I'm yours."
"I didn't realize you were such a romantic, Luke." My heart felt like it was soaring. "How did I get so lucky?"
"I think the question is how did we get so lucky?" He grabbed my hand and we ran up the stairs to his bedroom. I pulled my top off as soon as we got to his room and I reached over and pulled his shirt off.
"Have you thought about…" he continued and I put my fingers against his lips.
"Ssh." I reached for his belt buckle and he took my finger into his mouth and sucked.
"Oh Luke." I groaned as he ripped off my bra and I reached into his pants. "I see you're happy to see me."
"Oh Lexi." He grinned. "When will you learn? I'm always happy to see you."

Epilogue

3 Months Later
Bryce

"I don't know what I'm going to do without you guys in town." I heard my words come out in a choked tone. "You know that you are rendering me practically helpless."
"You're not helpless, papa Brycey." Shelby grabbed a hold of my leg, grinning at me. I picked her up and held her close to me. Her blonde hair was finally growing out and she had put on some weight. She was starting to look like the healthy, normal little girl she was now.
"Remember that, Shelby." I kissed her cheek and put her back down. "Why don't you go and play with Bongo?"
"Bongo wants a hug?" she asked me with open, excited eyes.
"Maybe just a small one. No suffocating him this time."
"Yes papa." She ran away and went to find Bongo.
"You're so good with her, Bryce." Lexi linked her arm through mine. "She's so lucky to have a dad like you."
"Well, I don't know about that," I laughed self-consciously. "I am sure she would like her big brother and sister here too."
"We'll be back to visit soon and we'll Skype every week." Lexi looked at me with tears in her eyes.
"Oh Lexi, don't cry. I'm just joking. I'm happy for you both."
"Bryce, you know better than to tell Lexi to stop crying. She's a crying machine." Luke grinned at me as he continued packing a suitcase. "Anyways you and Shelby have to come visit us soon anyways so you can try on the suit and stuff."

"Don't remind me. I need to work out. You can't have the best man looking like a chunky monkey."
"You trying to upstage me on my wedding day, bro?"
"Not quite." I laughed. "I don't think I can do that, even if I try."
"I only have eyes for you, Luke." Lexi cut in and Luke groaned.
"Uh huh."
"Luke." Lexi hit him in the arm and I watched as he pulled her towards him for a long kiss. I grinned as they kissed and looked away. I was so happy that my history with Lexi hadn't made this awkward. I was so lucky that I had a brother that was pretty levelheaded and cool. It felt weird to think that I had a brother. But I felt like he had been another blessing in my life. "Thank you, mom." I whispered, content.
"So, Bryce, don't forget to get a baby sitter for that weekend. We are going to have the bachelor party to end all bachelor parties." Luke winked at me and I laughed.
"Your fiancée may not like that, bro."
"I think I'll trust you, Bryce." She grinned. "I know you won't let your brother get into too much trouble."
"Well, you know. We have to make up for lost years." I high fived Luke and Lexi rolled her eyes.
"My mom and dad said that you and Shelby are to come over for lunch every Sunday," Luke laughs and changes the subject. "Let's not get me into trouble before I'm even married."
"I suppose they'll expect me to go to church with them as well?" I groaned but I feel a warm glow inside. This was what a family was meant to feel like.
"You know they've already signed Shelby up for Sunday School." Luke laughed and I groaned.

“I guess I better brush up on my bible verses.”
“God made the world in seventy days, papa.” Shelby jumped up and down and I groaned.
“I guess I need to start those classes soon.” I made a face and Lexi started laughing.
“Seven days, Shelby, seven days.” I tried not to laugh as I corrected her. I already knew the reverend was going to have a hey day with us.
“And then there was a big bang bang.” Shelby ran around, screaming and shouting “bang bang” and we all burst out laughing.
“You’re a good dad, Bryce.” Lexi whispered in my ear. “I’m so proud of you.”
“I just hope I can raise her right.” I whispered back, gratefully.
“The judge knew what he was doing when he signed off on the paperwork, Bryce. Remember that.” She smiled at me sweetly and I kissed her cheek.
“Thank you, Lexi.” We stared at each for a few moments, both of us letting our love shine through. I was thankful every day that I woke up and realized I had a friend like Lexi in my life. It was almost a joke to us both now that she had been so in love with me in high school. We were like brother and sister most of the time, bickering over every little detail. It was almost ironic how little we had in common. But I was thankful for her crush, because it had led to me having the life most men could only dream of.
I watched as Lexi and Luke touched each other as they packed. I see the furtive and passionate glances they exchanged and I delighted at seeing such a perfect couple together. It’s funny how life can work sometimes. I had thought I needed to stay with Lexi to feel complete and loved and to prove I was a man worthy of love, but it was

our giving up that dream and facing reality that had proven to give us the greatest gift and love of all. I understood now what people meant by letting go. Sometimes, letting go of love gave you an even greater one.
Ding-dong. “That must be Anna, will you get it Bryce?” Lexi asked me, pulling away slightly from Luke’s embrace and I rolled my eyes as I walked towards the door. I felt excited as I walked to the door. I’d only seen Anna a few times in the last few months but each time had seemed magical and I was anxious to see her again.
“Hey gorgeous.” I opened the door and stared at Anna. She look as she always did to me now, beautiful, calm, sweet and witty. She gave me a wide smile and poked me in the arm as I hugged her.
“I see you’re still lying,” she grinned but I could tell she was happy to see me as well. I wanted to grab her hand and kiss it. I wanted to just touch her and be touched by her. Every time I felt her close to me, I felt even more alive.
“It’s good to see you.” I tried to let my words convey how much she meant to me.
“You too.” She nodded as we walked back to the living room, where Luke and Lexi were packing their suitcases.
“When do you start classes for your Vet program?” I didn’t want to end our conversation. I wanted to ask her what was new in her life. I wanted to find out if she is seeing anyone.
“Next semester. What about you? Have you decided what classes you’re going to take?”
“I’m going to take some classes online.” I smiled. “I’ll be working for Luke here in Jonesville, selling software and stuff. So I’m going to take some computer classes.”
“Oh, a regular family business, huh?” She laughs and I join her.
“Who knew, right?” I felt warm inside. It was warmth I

don't remember feeling since I was a young child. I looked at Luke as he packed and I felt an overwhelming sense of pride and joy. He was my little brother but he was soo much more than that. I felt like a better man just for knowing him.

"Hey Anna." Lexi rushed over and gave her a big hug. "I'm so glad you made it."

"Are you joking? I can't miss my best friend's big departure to Los Angeles." She grinned but I could see sadness in her eyes. The same sadness I had felt inside but tried to hide. I knew that they were talking again but I knew they weren't as close as they used to be. And that made me sad. I felt like I was responsible for ruining their friendship, even though Lexi told me that a fracture was inevitable. I was just the catalyst to the explosion that was already coming, she had said.

"You guys will have to come visit us." Luke tried to prevent a tear fest from happening. "We got awesome housing at UCLA. Close to campus for me and close to the production company Lexi will be working at."

"What will you be doing there, Lexi?" Anna asked her curiously. "I thought you were hoping to act."

"I am," Lexi grinned. "But I figure I should get some other skills as well, just in case I suck." We all laughed at her words. I was sure she would make a great actress but I'm sure every other wannabe actress's family felt the same thing.

"I can't believe you guys are moving." Anna bit her lip. "I can't believe you're not going to MIT either, Luke."

"I tried to convince him," Lexi groaned. "But he had already applied to UCLA."

"They had a great program." He grinned. "And I knew you wanted to go to Los Angeles."

"But we weren't even a couple when you applied." Lexi shook her head.
"Maybe I'm psychic." He grinned. "It was inevitable that we would be together."
"I guess." Lexi walked over to him and he pulled her in for a kiss.
"Maybe you can drive Shelby and me to visit them, now you have a car?" I laughed and changed the subject and Anna grinned at me.
"If you're a good boy, I might just do that." She smiled and, as our eyes meet, my heart jumped. All of a sudden I wished it were just us in the room. I wanted to ask her if she would give me another chance. I wanted to know if she thought that she could see herself as a mother to Shelby and as a wife to me. I wanted to ask her if she would make an honest man out of me. I felt that deep, guttural feeling in my stomach and I knew, without a doubt, what Luke has most probably known all his life about Lexi. I knew that Anna was the one for me. I knew that there was no second best. There was no other. She was my soul mate. She was my other half. I tried to hide a sigh, as I kept quiet. I had to go slow, I knew that. But I also knew that I would do everything in my power to win her heart.
"Aunty Anna, Aunty Anna." Shelby ran into the room and threw herself into Anna's arms. Bongo came running behind her and crashed into Anna and Shelby, and I watched as they fell to the side. I rushed over to grab both of them and I could feel Anna's heart beating as I held her in my arms briefly.
"Thanks Bryce. You're a regular knight in shining armor."
"Anything for a damsel in distress."
"You are silly, Papa." Shelby laughed and patted Bongo's head. "Naughty Bongo."

"Do you remember how to get him to sit and roll-over, Shelby?" Anna bent down and smiled. "Do you remember what I taught you?"
Shelby nodded shyly and put her hand out. "Sit Bongo," she whispered. Bongo looked up at his name and jumped up with his tongue hanging out.
Anna whispered to Shelby, "One more time."
"Sit Bongo." Shelby's voice was firm and Bongo hesitated for a few seconds but then sat down. "Good boy, Bongo." She grinned and patted his head.
"I did it, Aunty Anna."
"Yes you did, wonderfully."
"Maybe you'd like to come over to dinner next week, Anna, and help Shelby and me a bit more. Now we're going to be his fulltime parents?" I asked her with my heart in my mouth.
"Sure. I'll even bring some special treats."
"Awesome." I grinned and I couldn't keep the excitement out of my voice. I didn't want to work myself up too much, but I really thought that there could be something really special there between Anna and I.
"Bryce, I wanted to tell you something." Anna walked over and looked at me with a serious expression on her face. "I don't know if you remember a few months ago, when you asked me if I thought you would make a good dad or brother?"
"I remember." I nodded.
"I wanted to tell you then that I wasn't sure, but I hoped in my heart that you would."
"You hoped I would?" I stared at her, confused.
"I hoped you would because I wanted you to prove my initial impression of you wrong."
"And now?"

"And now you've far surpassed anything I could have ever dreamed of." She smiled at me. "You're a great father and a great brother."
"And one day, maybe even a great husband." I whispered softly and she gasped and her eyes lit up.
"Have you heard from your dad recently, Bryce?" Luke looked at me with a concerned expression and I shook my head in frustration, slightly upset that he had ruined my moment with Anna.
"I think he's in South America. Once David told him about all the evidence we had piled up on him, he quit and left. For good."
"Good riddance," Lexi said, softly, before looking at me. "Sorry."
"Don't be sorry. I have my real family. That's all I need."
"Can you believe it?" Lexi laughed, "We're all kinda related."
"Thanks to Shelby," Luke grinned and rubbed her hair.
"Do I get a candy?" she grinned. "Please?"
"No, sweetheart." Lexi picked her up. "But you get something even better. You get the three of us, all here to love you for the rest of your life." She kissed Shelby's cheek and then looked at Anna. "Actually," she grinned, "You get all four of us. For a lifetime."
"And I get to be your flower girl too, right?" She danced around excitedly. "I get to throw flowers."
"Yes, my love. We're all one big happy family now."
"My own forever family?" Shelby looked around the room and grinned before running back to me. "And you're my papa." I picked her up and held her close.
"I'm your papa, your brother, your Brycey, your everything, darling. I'm anything and everything you want me to be."

"I love you, Papa."
"I love you too, my darling."
"You made all my dreams come true, Papa," she whispered into my ear and I felt the tears prick my eyelids.
"And you made all my dreams come true as well, my beautiful girl. You healed my broken heart, my love. You healed my broken heart."

Thank you for reading 'Healed,' the sequel to 'Scarred'. I hope you enjoyed it. Feel free to leave a review and share the book with your friends.

My next book 'The Last Boyfriend' will be out on April 15th 2013.

Please join my mailing list at:
http://jscooperauthor.com/mail-list
so that you can be notified whenever I have a new release. I would also love for you to like my Facebook page at:
http://www.facebook.com/J.S.Cooperauthor
and tell me what you thought of the book.

BONUS

Do you want to hear the song Luke sang to Lexi? Then go to *http://jscooperauthor.com/healed-lukes-song-to-lexi*

CPSIA information can be obtained at www.ICGtesting.com
Printed in the USA
LVOW10s1711220115

423935LV00009B/1069/P